Treasures
of
Many

A New World

Book 1

Jonathan Glaude

The songs are in no way a copyright of this book, all rights belong to the original song writers.

Text copyright © 2020 by Jonathan Glaude
Illustrations copyright © 2020 by Jonathan Glaude
Editor 2020 by Opalina Wolfsmoon

Printed in the United States of America
First Printing, 2020
ISBN 978-0-578-71557-5

https://treasureofmany.com/

In dedication to Robert, Joseph, and Presley.

Thank you for being you!

Dreams are more than just an idea, it's inspiration for greatness!

A big thank you to the following music artists who have helped shape my book into something better!

1. Arrogant Worms - The Last Saskatchewan Pirate
2. Ima - Que Sera Sera
3. Kongos - Come with Me Now
4. Pitbull - Timber (feat. KeSha)
5. Leo Morachioli - Baby Shark (Metal Version)
6. Dirty Heads- Cabin by the Sea.
7. Lindsey Stirling - Crystallize
8. The xx- Crystalised
9. Fleetwood Mac - The Chain (2004 Remaster)
10. Patty Gurdy - The Longing (Hardy Gurdy Version)

YouTube playlist can be found under

"Treasures of Many"

Treasures
of
Many

A New World

Book 1

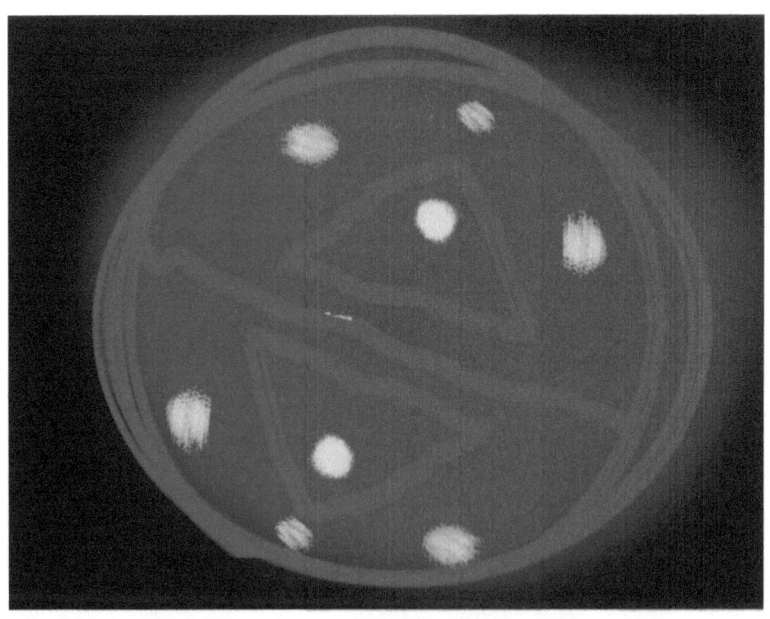

Chapter 1

The Lighthouse

A Dark and Stormy Night

Tommy is a ghost boy about eight years old, and Bahrk is a small skeleton dog, a miniature schnauzer to be exact. They were laying in a field wondering what they should do. "It's getting dark and windy out here Bahrk, and it looks like it's about to start raining too. Where do you think we should go," Tommy asked? "Bark, bark," barked Bahrk. "Hey, you found a lighthouse, but it looks old and run-down," Tommy said. Even so, Tommy couldn't resist exploring the lighthouse, so off he went while yelling, "let's go, Bahrk!"

As they ran through the field of tall grass, Tommy wondered how it was getting windy and stormy so quickly. They reached the lighthouse, and Tommy noticed the door was open. "Hello," Tommy asked? There was no answer, the lighthouse looked empty, so Tommy tried again, "hello, is anyone there?" Suddenly they heard a man's voice say, "no, go away."   "That's odd," said Tommy.

All of a sudden, Bahrk barked. "What is it, boy," Tommy asked? "Bark, bark," answered Bahrk. "Oh, you see a ship way out at sea," Tommy said. It was so dark that Tommy could barely see the ship but he could hear the bell on the ship. "Why isn't the light in the lighthouse on Bahrk,"

Tommy asked? "Let's go see if we can turn it on for the ship." Tommy, went back to the door and said, "could you turn on the light for the ship?" There was no answer. "Hello," Tommy asked confused?

Tommy and Bahrk entered the lighthouse and started climbing the stairs. It was kind of spooky inside with cobwebs and empty crates scattered throughout the inside, but Tommy didn't mind because Bahrk led the way. Bahrk, of course was brave, and he was always happy to go first.

At the top of the stairs, Tommy and Bahrk found the light. They walk into the Lantern Room, and the light was not on. While looking around, they saw a glass door that led outside to the balcony. They stepped out and could hear the ship getting closer. The wind was blowing harder now, and the rain was pounding down. The wind was so strong it almost blew Tommy and Bahrk away.

"Bahrk, the ship is getting closer, and is coming this way. We need to turn on the light," Tommy yelled! Going back inside, they looked around the room to find a way to turn on the light. "Flip the red lever or Pull the red lever down," said the mysterious voice. It was the spirit voice again. Tommy looked around and could not see anyone. Since Tommy is a ghost, which is similar to a spirit, he could not understand why the spirit behind the voice would not show itself. He chalked it up to the voice being the spirit of the lighthouse, who did not have a ghost body.

Looking outside, Bahrk and Tommy saw that the ship was getting closer and closer. Tommy was beginning to hear faint voices from the crew on the ship. He couldn't quite make out what they were saying, but Tommy realized they did not have much time. Turning to Bahrk, Tommy asked, "quick, what switch did the voice say Bahrk?" Bahrk walked over to the door and barked a few times. "No Bahrk," Tommy said with quickness in his voice. "Where were you when the voice said to turn on the switch?" Bahrk ran to the opposite end of the room, away from the ocean, next to a panel. There, in the middle of the panel, was a big red lever. "That must be the lever Bahrk!" said Tommy. Tommy tried to pull the lever down, but he couldn't. "It's stuck Bahrk, can you help me," Tommy screamed with panic in his voice? Bahrk went over to the lever. He grabbed it with his teeth, and together they pulled down as hard as they could. "It's moving," exclaimed Tommy! Suddenly, the light turned on. "It's working, it's working," Tommy yelled with excitement! Finally, the light started spinning around.

The beam of light was so bright, Tommy could now see people jumping and running around on the ship. Tommy also could see the pirate flag on the mast. The flag was a big black sail with a skull wearing a captain's hat and crossbones. He could hear some of what the crew was saying, "helm, helm, turn port, turn port!" Tommy wondered what port meant. The ship started turning left, away from the lighthouse. Tommy knew turn meant to move, so port must be left, but why not just say turn left? Now the ship was going towards the docks. Tommy knew that a dock is a wooden platform where ships can park in the water. Tommy thought about how he would like to meet the pirates, and why not, Tommy and Bahrk are brave! Tommy and Bahrk ran down the stairs outside of the lighthouse. As they were leaving, they could hear the spirit of the lighthouse saying, "thank you."

They ran through the field of grass towards the docks. Tommy started to get nervous as they got closer to the ship. He was wondering if the pirates were mean. He felt better knowing that Bahrk was by his side. Nevertheless, he just had to meet them. They reached the docks and walked closer and closer to the ship, gradually slowing down. Tommy and Bahrk reached the ship but were too afraid to go any further. They turned around and started walking away when they heard a loud voice, "ahoy, me matey! Ye be the ones that turned on that light?"

Tommy stopped; he was too petrified to go any further. "Who me," Tommy hesitated? "Arrrrrr, I saw ye runnin' out of the lighthouse." He was a pirate! Tommy slowly turned to the pirate and said, "yes sir," with a quiver in his voice. "Well, what ye be waitin' fer, come over here so we can thank ye," said the pirate. Tommy did not know what to think, but he was there and it would be impolite to run away, so Tommy and Bahrk walked onto the ship. Tommy noticed the man who was talking to him was wearing a big old pirate captain's hat. A captain is the man in charge of the ship and sometimes owns the ship. "What be ye name lad," said the Captain? "My name is Tommy sir, and this is Bahrk," Tommy quickly said. Bahrk barked a few times. "Well Tommy, come here so ye can meet me crew," said the Captain. "Ahoy me hearties, here be the lad who saved us, three cheers," announced the Captain. "Hip! Hip! Hora," said the entire crew!

"My name is Cap'n Samm, with 2 m's mind ye! This is Sarrah, my quartermaster.. Martin, Robert, Joseph, and Isabell, and the ship's name is *The Night Drifter*. Where ye from lad," asked Cap'n Samm? "I don't know sir," Tommy said, never having thought about it before. "Well, where be ye caretakers," asked Cap'n Samm? "Caretakers," Tommy asked puzzled? Tommy tried to understand what caretakers were. "Arrrrrr, ye parents or grandparents," said Cap'n Samm. "I don't know sir, I don't think I have any." Tommy wanted to remember. "Well, what do ye know," asked Cap'n Samm with a sad look in his eyes? "I woke up here in this field, and Bahrk ran up and greeted me. I named him that because all he did was bark at me," Tommy exclaimed. "Well, we can't just be leaving ye here. Why don't ye come with us," he asked with a smile on his face? "With you sir," asked Tommy almost in shock? "Arrrrrr, why not, we could use another crewman," the Cap'n said. "Well, aren't pirates mean," asked Tommy? "Only to our enemies," laughed Cap'n Samm! "Ok sir, but can I bring Bahrk with me?" Tommy would not go if Bahrk could not, as he already had a great fondness for his little dog. "Arrrrrr of course, the more, the merrier," Cap'n Samm shouted happily! "Well, in that case, we would be honored to join your crew sir," exclaimed Tommy! Happily, Bahrk howled in agreement. Suddenly, everyone on the ship started cheering again!

The Eye of the Storm

The ship was stocked full of supplies, and Cap'n Samm was ready to set sail. "Hands, hoist the sails, weigh anchor and hoist the mizzen" commanded Cap'n Samm! Tommy was a little nervous since this was his first time out at sea, and he was also extremely excited. He turned to Cap'n Samm and asked, "where are we going Cap'n?" "To find booty me lad," said the Cap'n. "How can I help," Tommy asked? "Stand back and watch me crew operate," the Cap'n said with a satisfied look on his face. Tommy found this rather difficult for him to accept, as he had a hard time to watch and not help out. However, he did as the Cap'n asked and watched as they rolled up the anchor, hoisted the sails, and tied everything down in a neat and orderly fashion. He noticed even little Isabelle, though younger than him, was helping in any way she could, and she was pretty good at it. Tommy was impressed at how well they all worked together.

They were about an hour or two out at sea since they had left port, and all seemed well. Tommy, Bahrk, and the crew were on course the Cap'n had set. Martin had taken the helm while Cap'n Samm was in his quarters plotting a course to his next destination. Robert started to talk to Tommy at this point, "Tommy, do you know the parts of the ship?" "No, I don't," said Tommy. "Well then, over there is the helm where Martin is standing. That is the wheel of the ship and the best place to see all around the ship." Tommy noticed the helm was in the back of the ship, and it was the highest platform. There was one higher spot, the spot was on top of a big standing beam with the flag on it. "What's that up there, where Joseph is standing on top of the beam," Tommy asked? "What, the crow's nest? That's where he watches for incoming ships or obstructions like land, rocks, or anything dangerous. The beam you are referring to is called the mast. It holds the biggest sails and our pirate flag," Robert replied.

"I remember hearing the word port in the lighthouse, does that mean left," Tommy questioned? "Why, yes it does. Starboard means the right of the ship, and bow means the front of the ship, while aft is the back of a ship," Robert explained. "Why not just use left and right," Tommy questioned? "That's because the nautical terms are better than using left and right; as it helps to avoid confusion. For example, if I say right, which right am I talking about, your right or my right," questioned Robert? Tommy had to think about it for a few seconds. There seemed always to be two lefts and two rights, but there was only one port and one starboard so he could see why using nautical terms was so important. "Oh, I understand now," Tommy responded.

"Do you know where we are going," asked Tommy? Robert thought about it for a minute. However, just as he was going to reply, Isabelle butted in, "I don't know but if I were to guess, only to the best treasure daddy can find!" Tommy thought of what treasure could be the best, wasn't all treasure great? He decided he would ask Cap'n Samm later when he came out of his quarters. Sarrah, who looked intimidating at first, walked over and said, "the Cap'n likes his special treasures because to him, any old treasure can be scooped up by a pirate, but the ones that are hard to get, that is what he is after." "What is special treasure," he asked? Just then, they all jumped as the Cap'n said, "treasure with magical properties!" They were surprised, except for Sarrah, as she seemed to know him the best and was looking in his direction.

"Treasure, like that blasted eyeball," Cap'n Samm exclaimed! "An eyeball," Tommy asked? "Arrrrrr, the *Eye of the Storm*. It grants ye the power to see through a storm," the Cap'n said seemingly upset. Tommy's next question seemed kind of dumb to him but he asked anyway, "why didn't you use it in the storm sir?" "Don't ye know the darn eye keeps rollin' away," Cap'n Samm seemed very annoyed by this but he shrugged it off. "Sarrah, I need to see ye," the Cap'n said, both Sarrah and the Cap'n when into his quarters.

Tommy thought about what the Cap'n said, he wondered if there was something he could do. He turned to Robert, "Robert, I wish there was something we can do to help him with the *Eye of the Storm*." Robert thought about it for a few minutes and said, "I thought about putting it on a pedestal by the helm, but it would just roll away in rough seas," Tommy thought for a few more minutes and suggested, "why not put it in a glass jar with gears attached to look up and down, left and right?" "Tommy, that's genius! Gears that won't move in a storm, I think I have something like that, gears we can use," Robert exclaimed! "Daddy would love it," Isabelle cheered, while jumping up and down! "Why do you call the Cap'n, daddy," Tommy said. "Yeah, daddy is daddy, mommy just went in with daddy, Martin is my older brother, Robert is the next oldest, and Joseph is the youngest brother," said Isabelle excitedly. "Now, you are the youngest brother with a pet dog," Isabelle could barely contain her excitement!

"Woah there, Isabelle! Me and Joseph aren't really the Cap'n's sons, but Martin is," Robert said. "Yeah, but you have been with us for a long time, so you are kind of like brothers." Isabelle just had to state it as if her life depended on it, which of course it didn't. "Joseph and I are brothers though, the Cap'n found us afloat in the ocean after pirates had blown up our ship. We were young, so in a way, we are kind of like family." Tommy had so many questions but didn't want to upset Robert. He did realize now, why Robert and Joseph had blonde hair while everyone else had black hair. "Ok, enough chit-chatting. Let's get some work done," Robert said.

"Isabelle, can you get the glass sphere the Cap'n keeps the *Eye* in and the *Eye*? Let's keep this a secret from the Cap'n until we know it will work, can you do that Isabelle," questioned Robert? "Yup," cried Isabelle and ran off. "I'm not sure that she could get any happier. She loves doing things for the crew, especially for daddy, the Cap'n that is! Tommy, you're with me," Robert said, while he tried to get over the embarrassment of calling the Cap'n, daddy. "I can show you around the ship as we look for the gears." A little while later, all three of them came back to the helm where Martin was. Robert with the pedestal, Tommy with the gears, and little Isabelle with the glass sphere and the *Eye*. She was looking so very happy because she was able to sneak it out without Sarrah or Cap'n Samm noticing.

Martin looked puzzled, "what are you guys up too?" Tommy was nervous about saying anything. "We are building a stand for daddy," Isabelle exploded! "A stand, well, I hope that works better than my breeches catching on fire again," Martin said. "Your breeches," Tommy asked? "Don't ask it's a long story," Robert butted in. "Too late! Yeah, I tried to dry off his pants with a new tool that Robert bought, and his pants caught on fire and put a hole in the back of them! He had to walk around for a week like that until mommy could make new ones," Isabelle started to laugh loudly. Robert started to chuckle when he caught the eye of Martin. "That's not funny Isabelle," Robert said being as serious as he could muster in fear of getting it from Martin again. "This will work this time," Robert said. "Yeah and how so," Martin asked? "We have Tommy," Isabelle shouted! "Well, if it works, it sure would make the Cap'n and Sarrah happy," Martin stated.

Robert, Tommy, and Isabelle started to work. "Get that gear there," Robert said to Tommy. "And that spring there Isabelle," Robert continued. "And If we added a crank to the pedestal, then it can look port and starboard and add another one for up and down," Tommy said. "Let's put that crank for port and starboard on the left; and then put the one for up and down on the back of the pedestal. That way, it is easier to tell which is which," Robert stated. Soon they came to a slight problem, the *Eye* was moving in the glass, in every direction. "Well, if we had something sticky to put on the bottom of the *Eye*, it would hold it in place," Tommy said. "Yeah, that might just work. I have something very sticky that can hold up to a storm," Robert bellowed. Soon it was completed, and it was functional. The pedestal looked great, but the true test would come in a storm.

Martin looked impressed, but he would never show it. Then, Joseph came down to see what all the fuss was. "Let's show the Cap'n," Tommy said. "Yes, but how are we going to get him out here without uprooting him from his work," Robert asked? "I know, I know," Isabelle said, starting to get excited all over again. "Daddy likes that song, the one with the farmer. Maybe if we started to sing, he will come out," Isabelle was ready to sing. "Worth a shot," said Tommy.

They all started to sing but Tommy, since he didn't know the song. *"I used to be a farmer, and I made a living fine; I had a little stretch of land along the C.P. Line, but times went by, and though I tried, the money wasn't there."* Tommy didn't know the words, but he hummed anyways, even Bahrk woke up and barked to the tune.

Just then, the Cap'n exploded out of his quarters and the door slammed open as it hit the wall, *"and bankers came and took my land and told me fair is fair,"* the Cap'n sang. "Now, what's all the commotion," Cap'n Samm asked? Isabelle was still singing. "Cap'n, look at what we made sir," Tommy exclaimed. Robert felt best not to say much until the Cap'n looked over their work. "Daddy, daddy, come see," Isabelle shouted, still all worked up from singing. Cap'n Samm walked over to the *Eye*. "Hmm, how does it work," Cap'n Samm asked? "You crank the lever on the left to go port or starboard, and the crank in the back makes it go up or down, depending on which way you crank the handle," Tommy said. "Good work ye've done," the Cap'n said with a huge smile on his face. You could tell he was impressed. "But will it work in a storm," he asked? Robert spoke up that this point, "yes sir, Cap'n! I have full confidence that it will work." "Well, maybe so, but we be goin' to test it soon," the Cap'n said. "Soon Cap'n," asked Tommy? "Arrrrrr, we are goin' to the *Isle of Stormee Weather*." "Where's that Cap'n," Tommy asked? "Not too far away now, we have been plotting the course," Sarrah piped in.

"We are about a day out and should get there by noon. So, we will rest tonight and be ready when the sun comes up," she said. Isabelle had lost interest in the conversation and started playing ball with Bahrk. "Tommy, come play with us," Isabelle cried. "Ok, ma'am," Tommy asked? "Please, call me Sarrah, there is no need to be so polite around me," Sarrah stated as she spoke in a kind tone. "Go, go play with Isabelle while we have the time," she said. Tommy went off with Isabelle, and together they played for a few hours.

By nightfall, there was a huge meal to be had that Sarrah and Joseph had made. They all sat down at the table. The Cap'n in the Cap'n's chair, with Sarrah at the opposite end of the table. Robert and Joseph on the port side and Martin, Isabelle, Tommy on the starboard side. Bahrk was under the table, waiting for scraps. The Cap'n took the first bite, "good meal me darlin'," said Cap'n Samm. Once the Cap'n had taken the first bite, they all began to eat. Tommy took a bit of food, and it fell right through him and onto the floor. Bahrk saw it and snatched it up, it went down and fell right out of his stomach too. Then he ate it again!

Tommy was embarrassed, but the Cap'n always had a way of making things better. "That's ok me lad , ye don't need to eat, after all, ye be a ghost," said the Cap'n. "In truth sir, I wasn't hungry to begin with," Tommy said a little embarrassed, as he tried not to be impolite to the cooks. "That's ok. Hopefully, you don't mind sitting with us so we can talk about the upcoming adventure," Sarrah said. "We be goin' through the *Chain of Storms*," said the Cap'n. Tommy liked being part of the crew, and wanted to sit and talk with them. He sat and listened as they spoke about the upcoming voyage until most of the crew went to bed.

Soon it was morning, and Martin finished his shift, so he went to take a nap. Sarrah was at the helm now. "Not that much longer now, Tommy," Sarrah declared. Isabelle always wanted to play and liked to play with Tommy. So, Tommy and Isabelle played until noon, and they stopped when it started to get windy.

The Cap'n came out of his quarters and said, "batten down the hatches! Secure the sails! Arrrrrr, we be goin' into the thick of it!" Tommy noticed that the storm spanned in both directions as far as he could see. "Tommee ye lad, the *Eye*, point it forward at all times," Cap'n Samm commanded. They reached the edge of the storm and trended in. Even though the *Eye* allowed them to see through the storm, it did not stop the rough seas, the wind, or the rain. Visibility was still very limited, even with the *Eye*. The water was choppy, lots of waves big and small crashed into the ship.

Tommy thought, thankfully I could not eat last night or I would be sick right now. The ship bounced up and down over the waves and through the storm. A bunch of crates let go, the ties holding them broke, as they crashed through a wave. "Joseph, Robert! Collect those crates," the Cap'n ordered. As Joseph tried to collect one of the crates by the edge of the ship, a huge wave crashed into that side of the ship knocking him off balance. Martin was on watch for any signs of danger and just so happened to be the closest to Joseph. Martin moved quickly towards Joseph, and just in the nick of time grabbed his hand. Joseph was dangling over the side of the ship. "Thank you, Martin, but can you pull me up now," Joseph yelled! In one heave, Martin pulled Joseph back on the ship to safety. "You're welcome, but be more careful next time," Martin yelled! Martin knew it wasn't Joseph's fault, but Martin was afraid he might not be there next time to help him out, after all, it was sheer luck that Martin reached him in time.

"Tommee, crank the *Eye* to the port and starboard sides, I need to get an idea of where we are," the Cap'n shouted. "Ok," Tommy shouted back and started to move the *Eye* towards the port side, there was no problem moving it to the port side. He then moved it to the starboard side. The Cap'n was impressed by their work, but there was no time to praise them. The contraption was working exceptionally well even though it was a very bad storm. Tommy noticed the Cap'n's smile, and was pleased about this and now he couldn't help but smile. Finally, they reached the other side of the storm. They saw not just one island but several of them, all in the middle of a vast ring of storms. It was so massive that Tommy could barely see the far islands. The water was calm in the center of the storm, and it was quite sunny too. "Head fer the big island over there, we be goin' to make camp there while we explore these islands," the Cap'n affirmed.

Chapter 2

Isle of Stormee Weather

The Hunt

As they waited for the Cap'n to make heads or tails of the map, Tommy decided to take Bahrk for a walk. "It's been a while since we have been able to go for a walk Bahrk, did you want to go," Tommy asked? Bahrk wagged his tail in delight. "Not so fast, me boy! Take this with ye," the Cap'n said. "What is it," Tommy asked? "It's well, it's, arrrrrr, oh I don't know, just keep it with ye," the Cap'n said aggravatedly. Tommy shrugged it off and slipped this round ball, about the size of a silver dollar into his ghost pocket. "Ok, we are off," Tommy said.

They started walking around the island and noticed there were trails. "That's odd, I didn't think there would be trails here. Let's take one and see where it goes," said Tommy. Soon they came to a point where there were five trails that met up, and Tommy decided to take the biggest trail with Bahrk following along. As it was just starting to get dark, they walked up to a clearing and saw a stone platform where there were treasures. There was a lot of it. "Wow Bahrk, look at all this treasure, I bet the Cap'n would love to see this!" Suddenly they heard a noise, but they couldn't see anything. "Quick Bahrk, let's hide." They ran to a bush just off of the trail.

A big wolf on four paws came running in, and then another. man-like wolf on two feet came strutting in behind him. "Look Bahrk, it's a werewolf," Tommy whispered. "We better get away from here and warn the Cap'n that we are not alone on this island." Just then, the wolf on four paws came sniffing. He smelled something slightly different. For him, it was a pleasant scent, but the scent of the stew was very overpowering. The stew was next to their beds in front of the treasure and a cooking pot with a low fire under it. Tommy hunched down and Bahrk mimicked him, staying very still, trying not to make any noises. The man-wolf said, "are you ready for dinner, Huck?" Huck, the wolf, pranced towards him knowing that he was going to get the big bone in the stew.

They waited quite some time, and the two wolfs were starting to settle in for the night. The wolf's bellies were full of the stew that they had and began to dose off. Night had fallen, and it was hard to see. There was only the moonlight, and that gave enough light but Tommy decided to wait a little longer since he noticed that the wolves were starting to get drowsy. The werewolf began to hum a little tune that went something like this. *"Que será, será, whatever will be, will be, the future's not ours to see."* The song came on strong at the beginning but slowed and became harder to hear as they were falling into a deep sleep.

Tommy thought this was the best time to get away. "Let's go Bahrk, I think we can slip away unnoticed." They slowly crept out from the brush and sneaked away, but Bahrk couldn't help but notice a bone on the side of the trail. He became extremely excited and tried to grab it. BANG! Bahrk hit the side of a tree with his new bone, and it made quite the noise, loud enough for the other two to hear. Huck jumped up suddenly, and he let out an awful howl. "Hurry Bahrk," Tommy said desperately, we can't let them find the others. They started running, however, Tommy did not recognize the paths at all since had it gotten dark.

They did manage to find where the five trails met up. Tommy did not know which one to take, but he had very little time to decide, so he took the left path. "This must be it." They continued to run when suddenly; Tommy fell into a hole that they couldn't see. It was a big trap placed in the center of the trail covered by vegetation. Tommy fell in, but since he is a ghost, he didn't disturb the covering of the trap. He could see a little light coming through the leaves that was hiding the hole in the first place. He could still hear Bahrk, who stopped immediately when Tommy disappeared. "Quick Bahrk, go hide," Tommy snapped at Bahrk. He was afraid that the wolves were getting to close. Bahrk whimpered a little but did as Tommy said and hid in a big bush, but the wolves never came.

After about fifteen to twenty minutes of waiting, Tommy called to Bahrk, "Bahrk, Bahrk, are you there boy?" Bahrk came running back. He pushed back some of the leaves, enough to make a hole for his head to fit in. "Help me get out of here! Can you find a stick that I can use to climb up with," Tommy asked? Bahrk was great at finding sticks. It was his favorite hobby. He came back with the biggest he could pull, being a miniature schnauzer had its difficulties though, as he was dragging a stick almost as long as him. Tommy reached for the stick and asked Bahrk to pull. "PULL BOY, PULL," he cried! Bahrk was too small, and the hole was too deep for him to climb out. Tommy could not decide what to do, but he knew he needed the Cap'n. "Bahrk, go get the Cap'n and bring him here," Tommy instructed. Bahrk was happy to oblige, so he ran off to find the ship.

Tommy heard footsteps getting closer and closer. He wasn't sure whose footsteps they were since it was only about an hour, if he had to guess, since Bahrk left. The leaves were lifted, and he could see a man. He was dressed sharply in a black suit, purple shirt, and he even had on a dark purple tie. "Well now, look what I have caught," he said. "Who are you," Tommy asked? "Who am I, who are YOU," the man asked? "I'm Tommy, can you help me get out of here?" "Sure I will," the man said. "Thank you," Tommy replied. The man dropped a ladder down, and Tommy climbed out.

"Thank you for your help sir, but I must be going," Tommy said. "NOT SO FAST," the man roared! Tommy did not want to find out why and tried to run, but he couldn't. "I can't move! How are you doing this," Tommy cried? "Magic," the man said. "There is lots of magic in this world, and I just so happen to have one ring that can stop people, even ghosts from moving," he said. "But I need to be going," Tommy shouted! "I don't think so," the man said. "A ghost boy would sell for a high price on the black market." "Sell me," Tommy exclaimed! "Do you know what people would offer me for a boy ghost that can walk through walls and steal any item they want? No, you are coming with me, let's go," the man commanded. Tommy didn't want to move, but he couldn't help it he just followed the man. He tried to turn and run in the opposite direction, but his legs just walked behind the man.

They came to a cave, and the man demanded that he walk in. Tommy hesitated, but the man shouted, "IN!" Even though he didn't want to go in his little legs obeyed and he walked into the cave. There were winding turns and twists, and the maze of caves just kept going deeper. The man knew where he was going, and Tommy reluctantly followed. Soon, they came to a well-lit opening with a cage against one side of the cave wall. The man again demanded, "IN!" And again, Tommy's little legs walked right into the cage. The cage door slammed behind him. "My name is Reeds. In time you will see what a great master I am but for now, you stay here. You wander off, and the cave monsters are going to eat you! HAHAHA," the man laughed as he walked away. Tommy wasted no time in trying to find a way out of the cage.

He tried to fit through the bars, but he got zapped every time he tried, and it hurt each time. What type of cage is this, he thought? Tommy was worried he was going to be sold to the highest bidder, or he was going to be forgotten and left here forever. He looked to see if there was anything he could use to help get himself out, but the walls where too thick for him to get through. There was nothing but rock walls and the cage. Even if he could get his hand around the outside of the cage, the lock looked hard to get at. After some time of trying, he finally gave up and slumped down. Just then, he remembered that he had something in his pocket. He pulled it from his pocket and realized it had a light scent to it. It was round and looked like it could open somehow, but how? He tried twisting and turning the round object but nothing.

Finally, he got very angry and threw it against the wall that the cage was near, and as it smashed open, an awful scent started coming out of it. It smelled like rotten eggs; trash that has been sitting for months and a man that has not bathed in years. If Tommy had a stomach, he would have lost it, all of it. "Just great, now I'm going to smell like that for the rest of my life," Tommy wept.

The Cap'n was getting worried. He had not seen or heard from the boy since last night. "The lad should have been back by now Sarrah," the Cap'n said as he was pacing the floor. "I agree, I feel that something has gone wrong. However, it's still not bright enough to go out searching yet. It just barely broke dawn," Sarrah said. "Aye, we will give it until we can see the trails, then I will go searchin'," the Cap'n said. About a half an hour passed and they could hear a bark, it was low, but it was growing stronger.

"There be the boy, Sarrah," the Cap'n exclaimed with excitement in his voice. "I wonder what tales he might tell us." Bahrk came charging through the brush towards Cap'n Samm. "Where be the boy, dog," the Cap'n was bewildered since the boy was always with the dog. Bahrk stopped for a second as if he was almost able to comprehend what the Cap'n was asking. "Bark, bark, bark, bark," Bahrk ran towards the Cap'n and then away, trying to get him to follow. "Sarrah, the boy should have been here by now. Something is wrong. I am heading out to search for the boy." Just then, a wolf and a man-wolf came charging in after Bahrk. Bahrk jumped swiftly behind the Cap'n and began hollowing.

The Cap'n shouted at them, "STOP! What be the meanin' of this?" "There are people here Huck. Thank the gods," the man-wolf exclaimed! The Cap'n stood cross-armed, waiting for an answer. "I'm Wild Wooly, and this here is Huck, my wolf," Wild Wooly said exasperated from running all night. "Where's the boy," Sarrah snapped? "What boy," Wild Wooly wondered in bewilderment? "Ye tellin' me ye haven't seen a ghost boy with this here dog," the Cap'n demanded, "No, to be honest, this is the first time I have seen the dog. We have been chasing the sounds of that darn dog all night. He has eluded us until this point," Wild Wooly said. "What do you want with the dog," Sarrah demanded with a fierce look upon her face? Wild Wooly took a step back afraid to answer her. "We were hoping to run into people. We have been marooned on this island for what we guess has been several months now," Wild Wooly stated. "And you are telling me you have never seen a ghost boy about eight years old," Sarrah burst out? "No, no, ma'am," Wild Wooly said even more bewildered, but he knew the type. If this was not her child, he was darn close to it. Just then, Wild Wooly said something he never expected he would say in a situation like this. "Well, if there is a lost boy then I will be glad to help find him, after all I have been here for a while, I know the island well. Huck can pick up a scent like it was nothing. He is the best tracker I have," Wild Wooly said. The Cap'n got to wondering what his angle was, but he did not have time to think about it. "Alright, ye help us find the boy, and we will talk about payment after," the Cap'n agreed. "Payment," Wild Wooly's mind was racing, "what would a bunch of pirates pay me for? he was thinking.Just then, the Cap'n had an idea about how to find Tommy. "Sarrah, I just remembered I gave Tommy a scent sphere," the Cap'n stated. "That's great, but did you tell him how to use it? Sarrah remembered the first time he gave one to her, he forgot to tell her how it worked too. The Cap'n's eyes widened. "Well, err," he stammered. Sarrah knew where this was going but was going to give it to him anyway. "No me dear, I sort of forgot," he said. "YOU DID WHAT," she screamed! Sarrah's face turned bright red. "We best be on our way me dear, we got a lot of ground to cover," the Cap'n turned in almost a sprint. "Let's go boys, we better hurry," the Cap'n and the others swiftly ran away. "Ye see a face like that, ye better start running for the hills," the Cap'n expressed to Wild Wooly. Wild Wooly couldn't help but ask, "why is that," he asked? "Well, there be no island left to search if she gets any hotter!" Wild Wooly almost started laughing but then looked at the Cap'n's face and started running faster.

The Search

They were midway into the closest trail that the ship was near, when the Cap'n pulled out one of his scented spheres. "Now you two mongrels, you get a good whiff of this!" He let Bahrk sniff it first. Bahrk kept smelling the item. Bahrk wasn't sure what to make of it as it had many different smells to it. Some good and some bad, but finally, Bahrk had it in his snout and started to sniff all around. Then Huck took a whiff of it, and he too couldn't make it out at first. He finally stopped sniffing it and walked next to Bahrk.

"Now then," the Cap'n started, "how did you find the dog," Wild Wooly replied, "we heard the dog at our camp." "Then we should start there and see if we can retrace his steps," the Cap'n said. Wild Wooly bucked a little, but he liked the Cap'n, so he brought him to his hideaway. "Now what you see here is mine, but I will gladly share it with you if you help me repair my ship," Wild Wooly announced. "So, that be what ye be after," the Cap'n started to get an idea of why he has been here for so long.

"What be the issue of repairin' ye ship," the Cap'n was questioning as they walked? "You see, when we came through the storm, we did not expect to run into so many troubles. We lost half the crew to the sea along with all of the repair materials; we have no nails to fix the ship or tools to cut the wood." Wild Wooly wasn't sure he could trust the Cap'n but he desperately needed off the island. "Alright, ye may have a deal goin', if we find the boy. I'll think about the fairness of it later," the Cap'n was wondering how much he could swindle out of him. For a pirate he wasn't cheap, but he did like to get a lot out of his deals.

"Cap'n, may I ask what those spheres are supposed to do," Wild Wooly was engaging in conversation at this point? "Well, ye see they be scent spheres. The part I forgot to tell the boy is, is if ye get lost ye are supposed to break open the sphere to release a smell. It can be smelled from a distance," the Cap'n started to explain. "How come you didn't tell him that part," Wooly asked? "I was too busy trying to make heads or tails of the blasted map." "Wait, you have a map of the island," Wooly cried! "This is great, now we can cross off the areas that we have been to find this boy."

"By the way, what is his name again," Wooly asked. "Tommee," stated the Cap'n. "Is it a treasure map Cap'n," Wooly asked? "Please call me Samm, with two m's mind ye." "Right, well Cap'n Samm," Wooly had to know now? "It is of sorts; however, it does not make any sense. The island should be twice the size judgin' by this map. There is no way of getting from the start to the cross, just a symbol midway in the map," Samm was getting frustrated just thinking about it again. Wooly wanted to ask more questions but thought better of it as Samm had a lot on his plate, especially with that female. Wooly started to get chills just thinking about what she would do to them if they didn't find this boy soon.

After about two hours of wandering around the island, the dogs came to a stop on the trail. They started pacing back and forth as if they had a scent but couldn't figure out where to go next. "Somethin' is strange," the Cap'n started to say. "Come on Bahrk, let's pick up the pace." Bahrk started to follow, but against Cap'n Samm's orders, he went right back to the side of the trail where Huck was sniffing. "There be somethin' that way," Cap'n Samm told Wooly. "But there is no trail," Wooly said. "True but look at the brush, it looks like someone has been walkin' that way, quite a few times I may add," Samm stated. "You're right Cap'n Samm. It's almost unnoticeable until you look past the trail," Wooly agreed. "Let's follow these mutts and see where they lead us," Cap'n Samm started to say as Bahrk took off. "Slow down ye mangy mongrel, I'm not as low as ye," the Cap'n declared.

They stopped at a cave entrance after walking a distance through dense brush, "we best be headed in as this mutt won't be waitin' for us," Samm started to say as Wooly butted in. "I'm not going in there. I won't go in," he said. "And why not," Cap'n Samm asked as he was getting frustrated? "The last time I made my way into a cave I was lost for days; my torch burned out, and I wandered aimlessly in the dark." The Cap'n started to gauge him as he said, "I see, a big bad man-wolf is afraid of a little cave, is he?" Cap'n Samm was poking at him. Wooly puffed up. "It's not the dark, it's the fact that caves have mazes, and the torches do not last long enough," Wooly stated. "HAHAHA, so ye do have some wits about ye," said Cap'n Samm poking him some more trying to gauge if he was going to be a burden. Cap'n Samm wondered if Wooly would decide to change his mind when he tells him the next thing.

"What if I told ye I have a special talisman that allows me to see in the dark," the Cap'n said? "Hum, you don't suppose the boy would wander into the dark caves all alone," Wooly asked still not sure if it would be a good idea to go in. "No, I think he would have turned right around if it started to get too dark, plus I can now smell it," Cap'n Samm said as he pondered the thought. "The sphere! Tommy broke it," Wooly said. "Alright I'm goin' in, ye stand guard out here and keep an eye out for danger." The Cap'n was now sure he was going into the cave to find out what was happening. "Wait Cap'n Samm, before you go, can I have that sphere just in case," Wooly asked? "It be me only one, but I don't think I will have a use for it in these caves, so I'll let ye hold on to it for now," the Cap'n said.

Bahrk went charging in. He stopped at every fork in the cave and took a sniff around. This went on for several stops until they reached a well-lit area. At this point, the smell was overwhelming that Cap'n Samm knew they were close. "Slow down mutt, we don't know what we are enterin' into," the Cap'n said. Bahrk started crouching down as if to be aware of danger. The Cap'n pulled out his pistol fully aware that danger lurks around every corner. They came up to a big opening, and Bahrk started barking and prancing up and down. Tommy suddenly awoke at hearing Bahrk's excitement.

"Tommy we've found ye," the Cap'n exclaimed trying not to get too excited! "But what are you doing in that cage," the Cap'n asked him? Tommy started by saying, "We found a trail and saw a man-wolf and a wolf." "Never mind that lad, skip to the part where ye got locked up in this here cage and get out of there," the Cap'n said. "I can't sir," Tommy wept. "And why not, ye are a ghost, ye can surely get out of anything," the Cap'n said trying to assure Tommy. Tommy touched the gate, and a spark zapped his little finger. "I see, its magic. Where's the key," the Cap'n was getting uneasy? "The man that captured me took it with him." Tommy was holding back the tears the best he could in front of the Cap'n. Cap'n Samm didn't seem to be that worried. "Let me tell ye a little secret Tommy," the Cap'n said to him. Tommy was puzzled as what he could be planning to do to get him out of this mess. "Tommy, I have the key to any lock," the Cap'n said. "You do sir," Tommy was surprised at what that master key could look like. The Cap'n pointed his pistol at the lock and said to Tommy, "best stand back lad, I'm not sure what a magical pistol will do to a ghost boy!" Tommy swiftly moved as far away from the lock as he could. The Cap'n fired his pistol, and it echoed through the cave mazes.

Reeds, the man that took Tommy captive and put him in the dirty cave, could hear the pistol shot and started walking away from the sound. He was surprised that Tommy had been found and so much quicker than he had anticipated. Reeds said to himself, oh well, so much for that profit. Maybe our paths will cross again someday boy. You better have your wits about you next time. I play for keeps every time, mu-ha-ha! He started whistling to himself while he walked further into the maze.

"Straight shot every time Tommy. This here pistol can fire through anythin'," the Cap'n asserted with a smirk of pleasure on his face. Tommy was astonished at the pistol, coming to the realization that somethings are not to be toyed with. "Remember Tommee; this be a weapon; it is not a toy. Toys are to be played with, but weapons be very dangerous," the Cap'n stated. Tommy was still amazed, as he nodded his head and opened the gate slowly. "Sir, can we go now," Tommy asked? "Alright lad, let me get me bearin's, that blasted mutt didn't give me time to mark anything." The Cap'n looked at every exit; there were more than he expected. "Cap'n, which way," Tommy asked? The Cap'n started out but then thought, which way should they go. Then suddenly something out of the corner of his eye caught his attention.

"Wait a minute Tommee. What is this?" He held his talisman up to the wall and could see a carving in the wall with a small purple gemstone in it. "I think this is what we have been lookin' fer; we better follow these mural," Cap'n Samm pondered. "But I know I didn't come from there," Tommy said. "I have a feelin' there may be somethin' I'm lookin' fer down this way," the Cap'n repeated to him. They followed the carvings from one fork to the next, making a couple of stops along the way, as there was a carving at each bend. They came to the end of the tunnel, and it opened into a significant cavity. Suddenly, the whole room lit up with fire surrounding every wall.

They both looked in amazement at what they saw on the wall. It was a mural. The most elaborate Tommy and the Cap'n had ever seen. Below they could see dark shadowy figures crawling their way towards the top. On top, they could see a teenage god-like creature casting a light away at the shadowy figures. He looked like he was holding them back. Tommy stared at the god. He thought that the god seemed oddly familiar; however, he felt it was his imagination. The Cap'n was studying it very closely while Tommy wished he could take the whole wall with him, it was beautiful to him. The Cap'n got closer to the wall, studying the god in the mural, and around the neck he could see a necklace. It interested the Cap'n. The necklace had a purple triangle. The imprint on the compass was the same size. He pulled out a fancy wooden object from his boot. It was long and slender, but Tommy could not see a purpose to it. Just then, it made a snapping noise and a blade popped out of it. It was a knife. "What are you going to do with that," Tommy asked the Cap'n? Cap'n Samm just hummed to himself and put the tip of the blade up to the triangle. He slowly took the purple gem out of the cavity of the mural. "Best not be tellin' anyone about this Tommee. I'm still not sure what to make of it."

Tommy nodded in agreement and said, he promised. They made their way back to the exit of the room, just then the room started shaking. It seemed like an earthquake. The ceiling of the room fell to the floor turning into rubble. It terrified Tommy. Tommy knew that he could not walk through thick walls like that of the cave. "Let's get a move on lad, I have a feeling we are not welcome here," Cap'n Samm shouted! They made their way to the first fork and suddenly realized that there were two paths. They were at an impasse. They did not know which one to take.

Wooly was waiting patiently at the clearing of the cave entrance. Both Huck and Wooly were sunbathing, like all creatures like to do, especially dog-like creatures. Stirred by the earthquake vibrations, they jumped up. Wild Wooly was no fool, and he knew that the Cap'n was in trouble. He was pacing back and forth as Huck sympathetically followed. He was determining if he should go in. Wooly then remembered that he had asked for the sphere. If anyone could find his way back, it was that skeleton dog, as he had a great nose. It was, in comparison to Huck, as Bahrk could smell exceptionally well.

Wooly quickly pulled the sphere out of his pocket and ran to the cave entrance where there was a stone, just tall enough for Wooly to crouch down. He scrambled for a rock. He found one slightly bigger than his hand and put the sphere on the rock. He went to smash it, but it rolled off. The rock where he put the sphere had a small decline. Trying a second time, Wooly was quicker and smashed the sphere. Huck ran to it and started smelling it like it was something he would like to smell again.

Back in the cave, while they were attempting to find their way, Bahrk started barking excessively. He caught both the Cap'n and Tommy's attention. They looked at Bahrk as he began to run towards the smell. They didn't know what was going on with Bahrk, but they knew they couldn't lose him. Bahrk was running towards this smell that he wanted so badly. It was the best smell he ever could dream. To him, it smelled like the best stew with the biggest bone he could ever taste. "Where be that darn mutt goin'," Cap'n Samm shouted? "I don't know, but he hasn't let me down yet," Tommy yelled back! Very quickly, they came upon the room with the cage. Cap'n Samm shouted to Tommy, "he may be onto somethin'! Don't lose him!" Tommy was running in front of the Cap'n. They were getting exhausted and it felt like they were going to collapse. They could see daylight at the end of the tunnel. "Look lad! We be almost there! Don't stop now," the Cap'n continued! The three of them made one last final push and bolted out of the entrance, where the two others were still pacing back and forth. When they were in the clearing, Tommy noticed the other two and shouted to the Cap'n, "they are going to get us." By this time, Cap'n Samm was out of breath and was walking towards the pair. "Slow down boy, they be our allies," the Cap'n was shouting to Tommy. Tommy looked for Bahrk and the Cap'n, he could see that they were puffing away and walking to the wolf pair. Tommy stopped and walked back to them. Wooly was yelling at the Cap'n that they used the sphere.

All of a sudden, the entrance collapsed sealing it off. The earthquake stopped, and they could finally rest. The Cap'n said to Wooly, "remind me never to be doing that again!" Wooly said with a smile on his face, "see!" Cap'n Samm stopped him abruptly, "don't be tellin' me I told ye so or ye may be gettin' a boot!" They started cracking up as they realized that they all just made it out safely.

Chapter 3

The Repairs

"Sarrah! Sarrah! We found the boy! Har! Har," Cap'n Samm shouted! He was walking several feet in front of the others when they reach the tree line. He wouldn't tell them, but he was excited to see his wife and proud of the others for the hard work they had accomplished, while they were gone. "That boy better not have a scratch on his head," Sarrah demanded of the Cap'n. "Of course not me dear. He is safe, and boy do we have a story to tell ye. Plus, how can he, he is a ghost after all," said Cap'n Samm. "Ghost boy or not he is still an innocent child, and you better well not forget that," Sarrah said with emphasis in her voice. "Yes, of course, me dear, not a hair was lost this time," Samm replied. "We saved the boy, and we even found the treasure, but I told Tommee not to mention it to anyone," Samm reassured her. "We will have to stay quiet about it for the moment. Now that we know it is real, if there is any more truth in the tales, then we could be in trouble," Sarrah stated. "Agreed," Cap'n Samm replied. By this time the boys had caught up to the Cap'n, and Sarrah was looking Tommy over, ghost or not.

"All right buckos, let's make our way to the ship and eat some grub. After that, we will take a look at that ship of ye's and assess the damage. I'll even put me best men on it," the

Cap'n said to Wooly. Tommy could help but ask, "how many men are you going to put on it sir?" "All of them me lad," the Cap'n replied while laughing to himself. "Even me," Tommy asked again? "Even ye Tommee! Ye can't be a member of the crew if ye don't know how to repair a ship lad!" Tommy was excited to know that he was included.

They ate and shared their stories with the rest of the crew. Little Isabelle was hanging on the edge of the chair the whole time and jumped off when she heard the part about the cave collapsing in. "That is quite the adventure you boys had. Let's not be doing anything as reckless as to that again," Sarrah said as she picked up her plate. "I can't wait for the next adventure," the Cap'n replied. Sarrah glared at him with that look, and the Cap'n quieted down knowing the next words were going to get him in big trouble.

Later that day, Wooly led them to his shipwreck. "There is my ship, the *Shanty Hills*," Wooly said proudly. "Sail ho," yelled the Cap'n. They reached where the shipwreck was, and the Cap'n called, "Joseph, any danger up there?" "We reached the shallows sir," Joseph replied. "Martin, careen the ship," the Cap'n hollered. "Sir," Martin asked? "We might as well be fixin' our ship too while we be here. It'll be dangerous waters gettin' out of here," the Cap'n said. Tommy turned and asked Sarrah, "what does careen mean?" "Tommy, that means we are going to clean the outside of the ship. We must remove the mollusks, shells, and plant growth from the bottom," Sarrah said. "Yeah, and daddy says he likes to eat the shells and mollusks raw," Isabelle blurted out almost in disgust. Sarrah leaned over to Tommy and in a low whisper said, "we usually cook them first." Sarrah chuckled.

"Alright men, let's get to work! Robert and Joseph get the tools. Ye too Tommee, give them a hand. Martin and Wooly ye come with me, we got to find some good wood to use. Make sure ye take the marker to select the plank size trees. Martin," commanded the Cap'n. After a bit of time, Robert and Joseph were cutting down trees to make the planks. They were going to use it to patch the hull of the ship. Fortunately, the ship was still in reasonably good shape even from the battering of the storm. Martin and Wooly would take turns cutting the wood with the other two boys. Joseph loved to dive into the water to patch the ship, so he was the first one in. It took a good long time, but he eventually patched the largest hole in the ship by the starboard side.

Almost half a week went by and they had the hull repaired, but they couldn't tell if water was getting in. The ship still flooded. The Cap'n turned to Robert and said to him, "go get the pumps boy, the buckets not be workin' well enough." "Sure. Sir, one of the pumps is in disarray right now and the other three work but are not working well, they need to be fixed," Robert said. "Then it looks like ye engineer crew better get to work on it fast boy," Cap'n Samm stated. Robert smiled and said to the Cap'n, "yes sir, we will get to work on it right away."

They were repairing the pumps in the hold when Wooly popped in and asked how it was going. Robert began by saying, "we got one open, and it is corroded." Wooly paused to think about it for a moment, "do you have any lime and salt?" They all paused for a minute to think about what Wooly said. All at once, they all smiled with huge grins. Isabel wanted to say something but ran off to the kitchen to grab the bag of salt. Tommy started running off to the island when Joseph called out, "wait up Tommy, we need to grab a few things first." Tommy paused and started to turn to Joseph. Joseph knew what he was already thinking. "The buckets Tommy," yelled Joseph. Tommy ran twice as fast to the buckets! Joseph turned to Robert. Robert took one look at him and said, "go, that boy isn't going to wait." Joseph bolted after Tommy. Robert looked at Wooly. "Thank you, this will make the job go much faster." Wooly replied, "call me, D.W." He said, "this might just work D.W."

They all raced back. Isabel was the first to get back, as she had a slight advantage. The salt was the closest to get, but she took it as a win. Tommy didn't mind though, as he said to Isabel, "I have the biggest amount." They looked at each other and said, "we both win!" Joseph chuckled and started squeezing the limes. Isabel was mixing the brine, which was a mixture of salt, saltwater, and lime juice. "Why do we need more salt, doesn't the water have salt in it," Tommy asked? Isabel puffed up and turned beet red. She was angry at Tommy for trying to stop her from helping. Robert looked twice at her and said to Tommy, One, it's to make it saltier than the water already is, and two, Isabel will kill us if we don't let her help." Isabel, who was listening very carefully to the conversation, jumped up and said, "exactly, see Tommy, Robert is always right."

When they finished the pumps, they raced them to D.W.'s ship. The pumps were working very well, even the pump that was seized spun like it was brand new. About an hour and a half went by, and they could see that the ship was lifted a bit out of the water. Tommy noticed a hole on the port side of the ship. It was letting in a lot of water. Robert and Joseph raced to patch it up from the inside. "There, that will hold for a while," Joseph said. "Well, what's that mean," Isabel exclaimed? Tommy was wondering the same thing. "What does that mean," Tommy questioned too? "That means that we will have to repair the ship from the outside," Joseph said. "I bet I know what she is going to ask," Robert said to Joseph. "Yup, and it's a no," Joseph said. "How do you know what I was about to say," Isabel puffed again? "Because you ask the same type of question every time," Joseph stopped his sentence waiting for the next words. "Well, in that case, I want to try next," Isabel was getting excited. Robert and Joseph belted out laughing. "NO," as they said together! Tommy was startled by this. Even poor Bahrk when he heard them, jumped back in a crouched position. "In that case, can I go," asked Tommy? They both started laughing. Isabel burst out laughing almost as hard as them. Tommy was confused, "I don't get it?" "You are the safest to go under the ship," Isabel said. Tommy paused and then turned to the other two, who could only nod because of their laughter. For the next few minutes, Robert and Joseph were trying to calm down, with only a slight fear that they would never stop laughing. Once Joseph calmed down enough, he directed himself at Tommy, "ok, hmm, follow me Tommy."

They walked to the outside of the ship. "We be floatin' the ship," the Cap'n shouted. All the men got into the water, except for Martin. He was with Isabel on the ship. The men pushed as hard as they could.Joseph looked at the Cap'n and was grateful that even the Cap'n was willing to help. They moved it just enough for Tommy to go under and repair the hole. "Alright Tommy, you head under the water with the hammer and nails. I'll be under the water with the wood soon," Joseph stated. "Drop the wood," Sarrah yelled as the Cap'n was getting out from the water.

Tommy went under the water, and something happened to him, he flashed back to something he couldn't remember before, it was his parents. They were looking at him, and there was a bright white light behind them. He would have thought that he would have a hard time seeing with the light so bright, but there they were. Tommy said to them, "mom, dad!" "We love you," they both said. "What, what's going on," Tommy asked them? "Relax son, you are ok. Oh, and remember to find your sister," Tommy's father said. Tommy nodded. "That's my good boy," his mother said. "We will always love you," they both said together. Tommy started to remember his sister and a locket.

Joseph was swimming down to the hole when he saw Tommy lying at the bottom. He let go of the wood and swim straight towards the Cap'n. He popped out of the water like a shark trying to catch its prey. "Cap'n! There is something wrong with Tommy," shouted Joseph! They ran as close as they could to see him. The Cap'n jumped back in and swam towards Tommy grabbing an air hose along the way. The Cap'n and Joseph tried grabbing Tommy but they had no luck, they couldn't move him out of the water. They waited a few minutes, trying to figure out a way to get him out. Tommy suddenly opened his eyes and began scrambling to the surface. By this time, the Cap'n was able to grab ahold of Tommy and help him up. The Cap'n didn't want to admit it but Tommy might have been helping the Cap'n out more. Out they all came. Tommy first, then the Cap'n right behind him, and Joseph last. The rest of the crew was watching, and cheered as they saw Tommy come up.

Sarrah came running towards Tommy, but as she tried to grab Tommy, she reached right through him. The Cap'n grabbed hold of Sarrah to stabilize her fall. "Careful me dear," the Cap'n puffed. It took them a few minutes but then they got their bearings, including Tommy who was still confused about what he just saw in the water. The Cap'n was the first to stand up. He waited for Sarrah and Tommy. They slowly came around too. "So there, Tommy, what just happened under the water," the Cap'n asked listening very carefully? Sarrah yelled at the Cap'n, "he just drowned! What do you mean what just happened!" The Cap'n turned to Sarrah, "he didn't just drown, he was under longer than any man could hold his breath." Sarrah stared in amazement at Tommy. "Tommy! You! You! What did happen Tommy?" Sarrah now perplexed at the situation. "I saw my parents and, and I have a sister!" Isabel was listening to the conversation from the window. She turned beet red again. Martin, now watching her from the window butted into her anger session. "And now you have a sister Isabel," he said to her. She thought for a moment and turned to him with a big smile, "Martin! We have a sister!" Martin chuckled at her. "We have a sister," he said.

The people near Tommy looked at the ship, including Bahrk, who was waiting by their side. "Alright, one more time, what happened when ye got in the water," the Cap'n questioned? "We pushed the ship, and then I swam to the hole. I don't remember sinking to the bottom but I do remember seeing my parents in front of a white light. My dad said, remember your sister, and now I remember my sister and a little of my parents," Tommy reminisced. Sarrah shouted, "what's their names?" "Mom and dad," Tommy replied. "I should have seen that coming," Sarrah said. The Cap'n started to crack up. Sarrah, who was slower to come around, started laughing too.

After a moment, the Cap'n exclaimed, "I think it be time for him to see the Oracle." Sarrah looked at Cap'n Samm and said, "I think you might be right." "Alright Tommy, no more water for ye, at least for the rest of the day. Sarrah, it might be a good time for some grub. Wooly help Joseph, Isabel help mommy cook, and the rest of ye," he paused, "keep up the good work," as the Cap'n finished giving his commands. He then moved to a spot where he could keep an eye on the two going into the water.

They had finished the work on the ships and were ready to go. The crew and D.W. all heard the bell and raced to the galley. The crew was all talking to each other as they swarmed in. They sat down and grabbed the food. It was a seafood chowder. "Perfect, just what we be needin' after a day in the water," said the Cap'n. Isabel started to talk to Tommy, "so, who is your sister?" "Umm, Alison," said Tommy, surprised that he could remember her name. "We do have a sister," Isabel screamed. Isabel was so excited that she almost jumped off the chair . "What else can you remember," Sarrah asked, becoming very much interested in the conversation now? "We used to play together all over the place. She is younger than me by about two years," Tommy remembered. "That would make her my age," Isabel shined at the thought of having a sister. "That be all good, but before we look too much into it, we better go see the Oracle," Cap'n Samm stated. "Who is the Oracle," Tommy asked? "You go to see her when you have lost your way," Sarrah said. "She will put you on a quest to find what you are seeking. In this case, it may be your sister," she continued. "But I don't want to leave," Tommy starting to well up. "What's the matter me lad," Cap'n Samm asked looking at him soulfully? "I don't want to leave you to go on my quest," Tommy said with a sad look on his face. The Cap'n started laughing, "it be not a matter of goin' on ye way me matey, but rather, us joining ye on ye quest."

"So, so, you will be coming with me," Tommy sniffled in excitement? "Of course, Tommee! We will follow ye through thick and thin." The three boys turned to each other and said at once, "yup, we will get the bottom of this!" Tommy looked at Sarrah as she nodded a little at him. Isabel was overly excited. "This is so exciting Tommy! Your very first quest! We are going to have so much fun," Isabel was shouting in excitement still! Sarrah started cracking up at her, and then they all started laughing!

After some time, the Cap'n turned to Wooly, "Wooly," the Cap'n said. "Please Cap'n, call me D.W," Wooly said. The Cap'n stopped to look at his crew, glancing at them all. Isabel looked at daddy and said to him, "what daddy, it's fun, Wooly always gets a new name. "D.W. little missy," D.W. said. Cap'n Samm chuckled a little and looked at the boys. The boys gasped! Robert spoke up, "I was busy working on the pumps!" "Why wasn't I told that D.W. got a new name," the Cap'n asked. The boys didn't know what to say and where dumbfounded at how they missed telling the Cap'n.

The Cap'n busted out laughing, "ye should have seen the looks on ye faces. Well now, ye will have to get a new name, now there Cap'n!" They all busted out laughing. The Cap'n settled down the quickest and said to D.W., "what are ye goin' to be callin' ye self this time?" D.W. stopped laughing abruptly, "oh, I don't know. I got to think of a new name!" They busted out laughing again. "Just be sure to add Cap'n in front of all the names!" Cap'n Samm was now laughing the hardest at the excitement in D.W. "Cap'n D.W. now, good sir," stated Cap'n Samm.

Two days had passed, and both ships had stocked for their long journeys. Cap'n D.W. called to them, "to my deck!" They all went over. "I have a parting gift for all of you. In each chest, there is a treasure as a thank you." Huck ran to Bahrk and dropped a bone at his paws. Bahrk started prancing with the bone in his jaw. Cap'n D.W. turned to Cap'n Samm, "your payment is in the two biggest crates, two magical mirrors." Cap'n Samm looked at him and said, "that will do me friend. Boys! Get these crates unpacked!" "They will triple the moon's brightness," Cap'n D.W. stated. "I will be hanging these mirrors right away. Give me four hours, Two hours to hang the mirrors and two hours to get ready to leave," Cap'n Samm said looking impressed with his newfound treasure. "You don't want to wait until after we are out of the storm," Cap'n D.W. asked? "I reckon it will be dark by the time we get away from here," Cap'n Samm exclaimed. "Good point," Cap'n D.W. said.

They hung the mirrors. Cap'n Samm said, "Martin and Tommy ye with Cap'n D.W." They both looked at him. "Yes sir," they said. "The rest with me, we are shipping out." The

Night Drifter went first into the storm, and the *Shanty Hills* followed closely behind. The storm was still terrible, and Isabel was in control of the *Eye of the Storm*. The Cap'n made sure she was strapped into the harness they made, that was attached to the mast. "Point it forward me darlin' at all times!" "Yes daddy!" As they trekked through the storm, they kept an eye out for the *Shanty Hills*. The *Night Drifter* came out of the storm first and watched as the *Shanty Hills* popped out. "Set a course for the Oracle on the Peninsula of Flume," Cap'n D.W. shouted!

Chapter 4

The Oracle

Questions Unknown

They reached the peninsula, and the two ships docked next to each other. "Now there Cap'n D.W., we must be off. We have lots to do," said Cap'n Samm. "Alright, I am off to find myself a new crew. Farewell," Cap'n D.W. said. After Cap'n D.W. said goodbye, Sarrah walked by and told Cap'n Samm, "Isabel and I are off to find more spices." "Have fun me dear," the Cap'n replied to her. "Boys, we need to be going," the Cap'n said. "Come with me lads, but before we be takin' off, ye must know this city is a lot rowdier than the last time we were here," the Cap'n stated as two men started fighting.

"*Come with me now. Come with me now. Boy come with me now, I'm gonna take you down,*" the musicians were starting to sing in the tavern. "Boys! This is what we came here for, good music and some grub. Get what ye want, it be on me tonight," the Cap'n said with a smile on his face. "Aye, aye sir," the boys said. The three older boys went off together. "Tommee, ye come with me," the Cap'n told Tommy. "We got some talkin' to do before ye meet the Oracle."

They sat down at a table, and a lady dropped a chicken meal and a mug in front of the Cap'n. "I remember you, you're not going to fool me twice," she said. "Then might ye point me in the direction of a treasure fool?" "That man over there." "Much obliged madame," the Cap'n said. He put a silver coin at the end of the table. "Ye think ye can bring him a stein little lady," the Cap'n asked? "Right away sir," she said as she took off almost in a sprint towards the bartender. She dropped the stein in front of the man. The man looked up at her. She then pointed to the Cap'n. The man got up and cripplingly walked towards the Cap'n and Tommy. "Cap'n Samm, I haven't seen you in a while. What will it be this time?" The Cap'n stood up and shook the man's hand, "this time, it would be pleasure." "Oh, in that case, you wouldn't mind me resting my old bones," he said. "Please take a seat, but first meet me newest crewman, Tommee," the Cap'n replied.

The old man looked at the boy and leaned into the table. He was looking at Tommy over, and over again. "It's hard to see this one," he said to the Cap'n. The Cap'n replied, "that's because he be a ghost." Tommy was unsure of what to make of him. He thought it was best to wait to see what the old man was going to say. "That makes perfect sense then. I was wondering why he was so pale after he's been at see for so long." "So, what did the Oracle tell ye this time," the Cap'n asked? "An old friend will be buying me dinner first." "Har, har, har, I bet she said that my friend, har hargh," the Cap'n laughed.

At this point, the old man started to sit down, taking his time. They took their seats, and the Cap'n announced to him,

"Tommee will be going to the Oracle for his first time."
"Where did you find him," the old man said to him? "We
picked him off the coast of Maria. Orphaned, that is," the
Cap'n said. "If he's a ghost, then his parents mustn't have
stuck around long," the old man inquired. "He's got a lost
sister, me dear friend," the Cap'n said to the old man. "I see,
mighty interesting," he replied to the Cap'n. The waitress
came over to them again and dropped another plate down in
front of the old man. "Looks like she knows your order," the
Cap'n stated. "I do come here often." The Cap'n looked at
her again and said, "much obliged madame again." He took
out a gold coin and slid it in her direction as he showed it to
the old man.

"Tommy was it? How old are you," the old man asked? "I
don't know sir," Tommy said. "Ha, the kid got manners. It's
hard to come across that nowadays," the old man chuckled.
"Aye, he be a good lad," the Cap'n replied. "Why don't ye
tell the lad a story of magical treasures," the Cap'n
suggested? "Oh, I have a good one for you," the old man said
as he lit up with absolute joy over getting to tell him about
the treasures of old. "There's said to be a treasure like no
other. It's in the land below. There are caves full of gold and
jewels," the old man continued. "Atlantia? My word," the
Cap'n said in a low tone. "Yes, yes," the old man exclaimed!
"I haven't heard stories of old like that in a very long time,"
the Cap'n exclaimed. "I have been saving this one for a long
time, a very long time. There is a jewel that contains very
powerful magic," he continued. "Much like the whole
kingdom," the Cap'n proclaimed. "But if you could find it
somehow, you may just be able to find the treasures."

"There is another story about the *Viridis Tropics*, a lost temple that is said to house the *Emerald of Nature*. The jungle is full of terror and easy to get lost in," the old man said while he was eating his turkey dinner. "Might ye have the map to this treasure" the Cap'n questioned the old man? "I might," said the old man to the Cap'n.

"Tommy, you will like the Oracle. She is very smart," the old man said. "What can you tell me about her, sir" Tommy questioned? "Well, not much. She usually tells you what's going to happen," the old man said. "Like a prophet," Tommy asked? "Something like that," the man paused for a minute. The Cap'n took this as an unusual sign from the old man. "What the? Don't be tellin' me that those old bones are taking the spunk out of ye," the Cap'n declared? "Just remembering the days of old, my friend," the old man said.

"It seems that my plate is empty. It's time for me to be off," the old man started to get up. It took him a little bit of time, but he got up. The Cap'n stood up and said, "hold on a minute, old man. There be a matter of business." The old man looked at him. "I thought this was for pleasure," he smiled. "I changed me mind about that," the Cap'n took out three golden coins. The old man looked at the coins. "That will only last me a month," the old man smiled at him. "I see ye will be lookin' for a nice bed this time," the Cap'n stated. "Well, these old bones won't be healing themselves any time soon," the old man joked. "Arrrrr, well then, it looks like three more may peak ye interest," the Cap'n looking at him square in the eye. "That will do just fine, take it as a discount for the meal," the old man said.

The Cap'n gave the old man the coins, and the old man opened a worn-out trench coat. He pulled out one of three maps. "Come back if you want another map," he handed the map to the Cap'n. He then hobbled away from the table and strolled out the door. The Cap'n slipped the map in his inside coat pocket and sat back down. He looked at Tommy. "That would be how ye do business with that one," said the Cap'n. "What's his name," Tommy asked? "The Old Man," said the Cap'n! The Cap'n sat back down and finished his meal. "We be off to see the Oracle lad." The Cap'n finished his stein and stood up.

They went some distance out of town on a horse-drawn wagon, so they would get out far past the great wall that surrounded the town. Past the fields of corn and other crops that were growing around the farms to the edge of the woods, there stood a lonely house made of clay and horsehair plaster. It was quite impressive for a house out so far. In the middle of the front portion of the house, there stood a tree. "Why is the house surrounding the tree," asked Tommy? "I'm not sure, all I know is the Oracle says it's a magic tree. The tree is supposed to help her with her magic. I never question these things," the Cap'n replied to him. They jumped off the wagon and knocked on the door. A little old woman about 5'2" opened the door. "Why Cap'n Samm and Tommy, I have been expecting you two. Please come in," said the old lady.

As they walked in, the old lady started talking to the Cap'n. "It's been a while. I trust you completed your last quest," she questioned him? "I did indeed," said the Cap'n. "Good, good, then is time for the next payment," she said. "Ten gold coins like always darlin',", the Cap'n suggested. "Don't you try buttering up to me. That silver tongue never works on me," she replied. "And the boy, five more for him," he suggested again. "Nope, you better try harder than that," she said looking Tommy over. She even grabbed his arm and lifted it. "So proportional and full of energy," she stated. "Five gold coins," the Cap'n tried again? She looked at the Cap'n, "double that and you may just have yourself a mighty fine deal." "That good," exclaimed the Cap'n? "That's nothing like what I charged you for your first time here," she exclaimed. "You are paying her, aren't you" Tommy asked while he looked at the Cap'n? "Oh, she charged me twenty coins the first time I met her," the Cap'n replied. "Well," she said staring at the Cap'n? "Of course! Of course! Yes," Cap'n Samm said. The Oracle was hopping around the room looking for something. "I'm giving him a discount since he is so young. There are not may youngsters that come by anymore, and I always liked kids." She ran up to the Cap'n and opened her hand. The Cap'n gave her the coins. She slipped the coins into her knitted sweater. She got closer to the Cap'n. "Well," she said, staring him in the eyes? "Well, what" the Cap'n replied? "You know the rules, in the kitchen with you. The kitchen is in the back to the right, in case you forgot," she said. "I know, though it has been a while," the Cap'n said. "There will be tea waiting for you." The Cap'n walked to the kitchen. She turned to Tommy. "Tommy, it seems you lived a very interesting life already, especially whenthe dirty man locked you in that cage of his.," she said. "I guess you are the Oracle, but how did you know that," Tommy gasped? "I know many things. Ha, ha! Nope, that wasn't it," she was still rummaging.

"Sit down," she said with her back turned away from him. "I will need that." Tommy looked, and there were two chairs and a table with a cup of tea on one side. Tommy thought she was sitting at the one with tea, so he started towards the other chair. "Not that one," she said. "How," Tommy was watching her the whole time and could not figure out how she knew what seat he was going to take? He sat on the tea side. "Ha, ha! Here it is! So, you have a sister, and she is still alive," she said. "I do," Tommy was puzzled about how she knew so much already about him? "Oh. Now, don't worry about it, you will figure that out someday. You got a quest to take on." She put down a box on the table across from him. "You will be taken far and wide to find your sister," she gestured to the tea and pointed down into the cup. "Look, you will see what you are looking for." He stared into the cup, and he could see a girl much older than him.

"There she is now," she said. "Who is that," Tommy asked? "Your sister. Now drink," she exclaimed. "But," Tommy started to say. She cut him off, "you should not know too much about your future. It's better to live it. Now you know that she is alive and well!" He did what he was told and drank. For some reason, the tea did not go threw him, he could feel it too. It was warm and tingled the back of his throat. When he finished, he asked her a question, "do you know where she is?" "I do not. It's your job to find her, but I suppose I will give you a gift," she moved the cup and put the box in front of him.

"What's in it," Tommy asked? "That's for you to find out, but this locket was your mother's. It's called the locket of two. It's part of a matching pair. There is a second part if you could ever find it. One was given to you a long time ago and the second to your sister," she replied. "How do you know that," he questioned? "I sent your mother on a quest to find them. No more questions now! You must meet up with your brothers soon. You don't have much time," she said as she started to hurry him along. "But, where's the key to the box," he asked? "That is your quest, find the key, and you will find your sister." She got up from her seat and shouted towards the kitchen, "Cap'n, it's time to leave." She waited a few minutes for the Cap'n to walk into the room. "What did you see," she asked him away from Tommy. "Tommee," he quietly said to her. "That's good. You must protect that boy," she said to him. "What about the items," he asked? "You will find what you are looking for in the City of Verdel. It's with a private collector by the name of Oscar." Tommy started to ask, "how do you?" She cut him off again. "I asked around," she started to chuckle to herself. "Now, off with you." She grabbed a ripped book and pushed it into the Cap'n. "Ye found the book, Treasures of Many," the Cap'n questioned while looking at the front cover. "Yes, yes. Only a part of it. as it has been ripped in three pieces. The boys are going to need you soon Tommy," she said to Tommy.

On the way back Tommy decided to question the Cap'n, "do you think Bahrk is ok in your quarters' Cap'n?" "Sure! He is probably enjoyin' a nice nap. Just wait, he will be a bundle of energy when ye get back," the Cap'n declared. They reached the town, and the Cap'n went to get the supplies for the next trip. Tommy went to find where Robert and Joseph were. He wondered around for a bit and saw them walking down a side street. "Tommy," Robert and Joseph said together! "What are you up to," asked Tommy? "We are going to get information about our uncle," Joseph said. "The Oracle said you would need me." "Huh, I wonder what she means. Well, why don't you come with us anyway? We are going to see a guy," said Robert. "A little shady if you ask me," Joseph said. "Maybe, but he is the only one with answers. He's a few streets down," Robert stated.

They walked down a darkened alley. Tommy started to get nervous. "Are we going to be ok," Tommy asked? "Don't worry Tommy, this is the black market. We come here all the time. Just be careful not to ask too many questions or they will take you for everything you have," Joseph said. He looked very serious as he was telling Tommy.

They walked up to a man, who was wearing a cloak, and all you could see were his eyes. "Back again," he said? "Do you have the information we are looking for this time?" "I might, however, you know the rules. No payment… no information," he said. "We have five silver coins for you," Robert said. "Not this time, it will cost way more than that. I have hit the big one this time. I have found what you are looking for and was able to confirm it too. So I know it is worth much, much more than five silver coins. This will cost you twenty gold coins this time," the cloaked man said. "Twenty," Robert and Joseph uttered! "We don't have that kind of money," Robert remarked. "What kind of information is worth so much," Tommy asked? "The location of their uncle. Now that is a nice locket you have there," the man said. "My locket, I just got it. It has a picture of my parents and sister," Tommy said. "It's very magical and valuable. It's worth eighteen gold coins. Even though that still isn't enough, I like the boy though, so I will give you a discount for that locket." Tommy looked at his new brothers. "Alright, my parents might be dead, but your uncle is still alive, he's more important," Tommy said. "Our uncle is alive," Joseph asked? "Yes, of course," the cloaked man extended his hand towards Tommy. Tommy gave him the locket. "You will find your uncle on Volcano Island. He has been there for a while, and he was confirmed to be there as of last month," he said. "Volcano Island," Robert and Joseph said. "Now it's time for you three to go. I have much work to be done," he said. He was looking at the locket over and over again. "Well, get going," he said. They looked at one another, and then started to head back to the ship.

"Martin! Arrrrrr, we all be here," the Cap'n questioned? "Yes sir!" Martin called to him. "Let's ship off. We got our supplies. To the City of Verdel," he announced to the crew. Cap'n D.W. looked over as they were heading out. Cap'n D.W. had a few more repairs to make before he could go.

The Needle

It took them a few days, but they reached the city in no time. "Now Tommee, ye with me. The rest go shopping," the Cap'n announced to the crew. "Yes sir," said Tommy. The Cap'n and Tommy took off first as the crew was resting for a bit before heading out. "Mommy, mommy, I want to go shopping," Isabel exclaimed! Sarrah leaned over at Isabel and had a big smile on her face. "Me too! Let's go," she said to Isabel.

Cap'n Samm and Tommy were walking down a street. "Now we be lookin' for a man named Oscar, a private collector. His place is supposed to be around here somewhere," the Cap'n was explaining to Tommy. "How 'bout we ask those kids," Tommy replied. "Best ye do that," the Cap'n said. Tommy walked over to the kids, "do you know where Oscar lives?" They pointed to a big mansion on top of a hill. The Cap'n looked up and had a big grin under his beard. "Thank ye me lads," the Cap'n yelled from across the street! "Let's go me lad, we got a lot of work to do," he yelled to Tommy.

They walked up to the house and banged with the knocker. The double doors started to open, and they could see a man dressed in a tailcoat. "May I help you," the butler asked? "We are here to see Oscar, we be here on business," the Cap'n stated. "Very well sir, right this way," the butler said. They walked into the house and down a long hall. There was a study at the end, objects and books covered the walls. There were stands with glasses in front of the bookcases. They all had magical jewels in them. "Please take a seat while you wait," the butler said. "Thanks, but I'll stand," said the Cap'n. The butler looked over at Tommy. He smiled and gestured towards a very elegant sofa. Tommy took a seat on the sofa and was enjoying how comfortable it was. Still smiling at Tommy, the butler said to both, "the Master will be out in a few minutes."

They could hear from the double doors coming from the right side of the room, "those are outrages prices," a man was yelling! A quieter voice said, "come back when you have the money." The doors opened, and the Cap'n could see weapons on the wall. An angry-looking pirate walked through the doors and stormed off. He was an elegantly dressed pirate, or so Tommy thought. A few minutes went by, and the butler came back with three teacups, a tray of biscuit, small plates with gold trim, and a gold trim teapot to match the plates. The butler looked oddly familiar to Tommy, but he couldn't think of where he would have seen him.

"Sir," the butler walked to the doors, and a man came out. He was well dressed, but his clothes were modern. "So, what is it I can help you out with gentlemen," he asked as he was rubbing his hands together? "Cold sir," the butler asks? "Yes, throw a few more logs onto the fire," the man said. The butler walked past Tommy. As he walked by Tommy, he winked at him. He threw three large logs into the giant fireplace. He then started pouring the tea. "We be here fer the needle," said the Cap'n. "The needle, oh yes, I believe I have that. The Oracle said that a distinguished pirate was going to be passing by," Oscar stated. "I see... so she sent word," the Cap'n said.

The butler handed the Cap'n his tea and moved on to Tommy. Tommy looked at it and then looked at the butler. "Sorry I can't eat or drink," Tommy said looking guilty. The butler looked at Tommy and said, "my apologies young lad." He then gave the master a cup and walked out of the room. "What may ye name be," said the Cap'n? The man put the cup down on his desk. "Oscar Michael Glaude," Oscar said. "What about you," he replied? "Cap'n Samm, with two m's mind ye," the Cap'n said. "The young lad," Oscar looked over at Tommy? Tommy stood up and said, "Tommy, sir." The two older men started laughing at his awareness. "You don't have to stand up for me, Tommy, enjoy that sofa you are sitting on," Oscar said. "Now then, you are looking for the needle." He moved away from his desk and walked over to a pedestal with a glass jar over it. "This was hard to find. It was like looking for a needle in a haystack," he joked. The Cap'n started laughing hard. Tommy looked at him puzzled. "What's the matter, haven't you heard of the expression looking for a needle in a haystack" Oscar questioned him? "No sir," he said. Oscar started laughing. "Well then, you should try it someday," Oscar replied. "Don't worry lad, we will try it. I'll show you how," the Cap'n said to Tommy.

"This will be sixty gold coins," said Oscar. "That would be all fine but the Oracle has already paid ahead," the Cap'n replied. "Although, I would be interested in some of those weapons ye have over there." Oscar looked at the closed doors. "Can't blame a man for trying. What can I interest you in," he asked? "I be looking fer two swords for right now… of the magical type," said the Cap'n. "How about a trade in the future then and forty gold coins? I may have just the thing, and they should be in any day now," Oscar said to the Cap'n. The Cap'n pulled out a small pouch and gave him forty coins.

Oscar finished his tea, and the Cap'n drank the rest out of courtesy. "If that will be it, I look forward to doing business with both of you in the future," Oscar said. The Cap'n looked over at Tommy, who was very much enjoying the sofa still. "Let's go boy," the Cap'n said. The Cap'n walked up to and put the cup and dish on the desk. "I hope this is alright," he said to Oscar. "Yes, that is fine," he replied. He reached over to the table and picked up a pendant. It lit in his hands, and a few seconds later, the butler came in the room with an object in each hand. Tommy started walking to the doors, but the butler stopped him. "These are for you," he said.

Oscar put up his left hand. The butler stopped and looked at him. "I'm giving him this toy," the butler said. "What's in your other hand," Oscar asked? The butler held up both the ship and an amulet. "Very well, if you want to give away your stuff, so be it, but I would charge him for that." "But sir, he is just a boy," the butler exclaimed. Just then, a girl with brown hair came in with a crying baby. "I need you to take him for a few minutes,' she said. "Meet my beautiful wife," Oscar exclaimed. "Would you charge your own son at that age," she scolded him? "Maybe, depending on what he has done," he joked with his wife over the crying baby. Just then, the baby was beginning to settle down. Oscar gestured to the butler while holding his son. "If you want to give away your stuff, so be it."

The butler leaned over to Tommy and handed him the two items. "Keep this with you. It saved my life more than once," the butler gestured at the amulet, "it's called the *planetarium clypeus*." The Cap'n stood up in surprise, "shiver me timbers!" He then looked at Oscar's wife. "How old is the lad," the Cap'n asked her? "Nine months," she said to him. "Well then, a favor it will be someday. Let me know when he gets of age to sail. I'll show him how to be a perfect quartermaster," the Cap'n replied to her. "Second mate," she said while pointing at him. "Yes, ma'am," he replied.

"We got work to be done Tommee," said the Cap'n. "Yes sir," Tommy said as he was heading out. He was happy to get the ship and show it to Isabel. He was hoping that they could both play with it when he meets up with Isabel back at the *Night Drifter*. The butler walked them out of the room and into the hall. "Don't lose that boy, whatever you do," whispered the Cap'n to Tommy. "Will do sir," said Tommy.

Back in the room Oscar asked his wife, "is that what you would like, my love?" "I've heard his stories, and I know his prophecy. Only the finest captain can put the pieces of the *Compass of Ginar* back together," she said to him. "Then, it will be done," Oscar replied.

Chapter 5

Piece 2

The Ship

Three days had passed since they docked in the City of Verdel. The crew was getting itchy to move, as they never liked to stay in the towns to long and much preferred the open oceans. The crew was waiting for Cap'n Samm's next coordinates. The thing is, the Cap'n couldn't figure out why the needle pointed down in the southeasterly position. He read and found the next gem he was looking for, *The Ocean Sapphire*. He found it in the back of the book on the last page, where the book had been ripped apart. So far, he had the *Viola* jewel and the *Needle*. All he needed to do was put the *Viola* jewel in the 12 o'clock position and place the *Needle* in the center. Sarrah came into the cabin and started to talk to the Cap'n, "the crew has already set sail." "What! What do they think they are doing," the Cap'n yelled? "I gave them the command," she expressly yelled at him. "What," the Cap'n couldn't believe it?

Sarrah decided to tell him her reasoning before he blew. "It has been three days since they have been in open waters, and they needed to go," Sarrah said to him. The Cap'n calmed down by this point. "Ye right, it's just that I don't understand why the compass points down on the face now," said the Cap'n. "Which way does it point," she asked? "In a southeasterly position," he said. "Does it all ways point in that direction," she was determined to get her answer from him? "Yes," he shouted in frustration! "Then we go to where it points us exactly," she was trying to comfort the Cap'n for a bit. "What if we need some supplies," he said to her? "Then, we go to the closest island and get what we need, or we just send for your new friend." "How do ye know that," he asked her? "I met his wife at the market," she said. The Cap'n gasped. "When Tommy had told me about her, I knew she was Oscar's wife right away," she continued. The Cap'n was intrigued by the series of events that took place with his wife. "How did you know who she was," he was probing for answers now? "Oh, someone that elegantly dressed and nice, there could only be one of those outfits," she said. "I should have known," he whispered under his tongue. "**Alright**, let's go," he bellowed to her.

The Cap'n came out of his quarters. He addressed his crew, "Avast! Good work! That be a test to see if ye can take orders from me second mate." The older boys looked up and shook their heads, while Isabel and Tommy were jumping up and down that they passed the Cap'n's test. Sarrah put her hand in her face, "can we go now?" "Let's ship out," the Cap'n commanded. They all cheered. "Martin, I want ye to follow this compass, wherever it may take us," the Cap'n ordered him. "Yes sir," Martin exclaimed! He was extremely excited about finally getting to use his father's (the Cap'n's) compass that he kept with him for so long.

Two weeks went by since they had been out at sea. Tommy and Isabel where fishing since they were running low on supplies. Martin noticed something funny about the compass.

It was now facing the other direction. He turned the ship around, and the Cap'n came out of his quarters. "What is it boy," said the Cap'n to Martin? "Sir, the compass turned," Martin said. The Cap'n raced to the compass. "Let's see that thing," he said. As the ship traveled through the center point, the compass flipped around again. "Circle the area," the Cap'n commanded! As they circled, they could see the compass move around in a counterclockwise position. It was still pointing down, but now it was touching the face of the compass.

Just then, a ship started to pull up from the ocean. "Prepare to fire boys," commanded the Cap'n. Tommy recognized the ship right away. It was the model that the butler gave him. "Cap'n!" Tommy ran to grab the ship and showed it to him. "It's the ship Cap'n," Tommy shouted to him! He found the ship and raced to the Cap'n, "it's the *Clipper*." The Cap'n looked at the ship, and sure enough, the two ships were an identical match. It even had the name of the ship on the side of the model.

"Beware Tommee, we don't know if they are hostiles," the Cap'n said to Tommy and Martin. By this time, the two ships were about parallel. The *Clipper* was pulling to the side of the *Night Drifter*. "Ahoy!" Boy, I haven't seen this ship in a while," the man said. "State your business," the Cap'n shouted to the other ship. "We are here to pick you up!" They could see an army of men on the ship, way more than any of them could take. "It seems you have us outnumbered," the Cap'n said to the other man. "We know. We have been expecting you. We are going to board your ship now," said the *Clipper* Captain. "Be warned, we are armed," the Cap'n announced to him, and as he was about to finish, the army pulled out their weapons. "Arrrrrr, I guess we don't have a choice," Cap'n Samm whispered to the crew.

The captain of the *Clipper* was the first to board, showing good manners and unhostile intent. He strolled up to the Cap'n where Tommy was still holding the model ship. Bahrk was barking and growling at the man. The *Clipper* captain did not seem to take notice of the dog and gestured towards Tommy's hands. "May I see that lad? You are the one," he said to them as he was looking at the ship. He handed the ship back to Tommy. "Now, if you may, we must be going. We are on a tight schedule," he said to the crew. "What be ye name captain," the Cap'n asked? "Captain William Ellsworth, Cap'n Ellsworth at your service," he said to them, with his fist closed and held up to his heart. Isabel thought it was a cool salutation. She decided to try it herself and mimicked his posture. He looked over at her and said to the Cap'n, "I like her; she has good manners." "Jimmy and Henry, you're with them," he commanded.

Two men walked onto the ship and started poking around at the mast. Just then, a small door popped open, designed to look like a crack in the ship. Henry put a pendent up to the gem inside the mast, and they glowed together. "Very well, it works. I will be off," Cap'n Ellsworth said. The Cap'n which captain returned to his ship. "What do we do now," Robert questioned Jimmy? "We follow. Pull forward," he yelled to the Cap'n. When the *Night Drifter* was behind the *Clipper*, the *Clipper* sank back down under the water. To the crew's surprise, the *Night Drifter* followed. The ship had a bubble around it so they could breathe. Martin was trying to get used to sailing underwater. Before long, they passed through a school of fish and sharks. They came to a city. The *Clipper* passed through a red-looking entry into the city. "We found it, Atlantia," the Cap'n Samm shouted! The water was below the city but deep enough to allow ships to float.

The *Clipper* pulled up to the starboard side of a long dock while the *Night Drifter* came along to their port side. The two finally docked their ships. The captains were the first two off the ships. Cap'n Ellsworth commanded to palace guards waiting on the docks, "see to it that they make it to the king in a timely manner." "To the king I guess," Cap'n Samm said to Sarrah. She was in awe of the city, much like the rest of the crew. Isabel couldn't resist, "I can't wait to play with all the royal kids." The royal guards chuckled while they were escorting the crew.

The Kingdom

"Welcome, my friends. I am King Bashiri," the King said, as they were walking through the doors. "I trust you had a fun trip," Bashiri continued. "Who are you," Tommy asked? "The King! Do you have a problem with that," he asked? "No sir," the boys all said at once. "We don't get many visitors down here," Bashiri said. "Are we captives," Sarrah asked? Just then, a woman stood up from her thrown. "If you were, you would be dead by now. I am Malikah, the King's queen," she said. At this point, the Cap'n was convinced they were in no danger. "How can I help ye good King," the

Cap'n asked? "You are here in search of something, yes," Bashiri questioned? "We are here for a gem. However, we cannot seem to find it," the Cap'n mentioned to the King. "We cannot go there, however, you may be able to," the King said. The King snapped his fingers, and a man came out with a map on a tray. "Sir," the servant said. "I expect you are looking for this," the King said. Tommy thought that the servant looked familiar but he shrugged it off. "This is for you, I expect it back when you are done with it," the King handed the map to the Cap'n.

"There are two criteria you must meet if you take on this quest. First, you must not kill my pet. Second, is you must get my trident above anything else." "What is your pet," Tommy asked? "Don't worry, he won't kill you," the King said to Tommy. "In that case, we will be off," the Cap'n said. "All of you," Malikah asked? "All of us. You wouldn't believe the type of trouble these boys get into," Sarrah said. "We will talk later," Malikah told her. The Cap'n and the boys looked at the King. The King looked at the crew and waived his right hand to send them off. "You will have an escort," he said. "May I suggest Cap'n Ellsworth," the Cap'n asked? "No, you will have my best warrior, Anik," the King commanded! Just then, a soldier came out. "Follow me this way," Anik said as he led the crew out of the throne room.

Anik brought them into the weapons room. "Now, you will all need weapons," he said. The boys looked around the room, and Robert and Joseph came to some fancy staffs. They both grabbed one. "Now those are great weapons boys. They work very well, but I'm afraid those will not work for you, at least the two you are holding. Try these," Anik said.

He picked the two in the very middle. They had strings of colors, like ribbons in the wood. They took the weapons, and they felt a warm feeling. "They are so light," Joseph said. "That's because these weapons pick their masters," Anik replied. "Magic staffs, we couldn't, they must be of great value," the Cap'n said. "It's too late, they have selected their masters," Anik said. "Let me see that Joseph," the Cap'n said. Joseph handed the staff to the Cap'n, and he dropped the staff. He then tried to pick it up but couldn't. "It seems Anik is correct. They did pick ye. Joseph, if ye may," the Cap'n said to the boys. Joseph grabbed his new staff. There was a slight breeze as he picked it up. The rest of the crew continued to look. Martin did not like any of the weapons. "Thanks, but I will stick to my swords," he said to Anik. The crew was busy looking around the room. Anik walked up to Isabel and pulled out a locket, "now little one, this is your new weapon. Keep it under your shirt, and don't let anyone see it. This will be our secret. You will need it when you are in danger." "Can I show Tommy," she asked? "No one for the time being," he replied. "Oy, fine," she said!

"What's the matter Tommy? Didn't you find anything," Sarrah asked him? "No, I don't like weapons." Anik butted in, "I don't think Tommy will need a weapon ma'am. His weapon is special. I saw the way your crew walked into the kingdom." "We were just protecting the kids," Sarrah affirmed. "Aye, the crew be his weapon," said the Cap'n. "That's what parents are for, don't you think? Now we must be going," Anik said.

They walked to a stable. "These will be your rides," Anik said. "Seahorses," Isabel cried. "Isabel and Tommy, you will be riding with Sarrah and the Cap'n," he said. "I want to ride with mommy," Isabel said. "Looks like ye be with me Tommee! Har, har, har! As he laught. These be not the normal seahorses ye see," the Cap'n laughed. "No, they are bred to be the size of your horses. Cap'n, it's time you looked over the map while we get ready," Anik stated. They moved off when they were comfortable with the seahorses.

Martin was at the end, trying to keep his horse following them. The horse did not seem to like being in the back but would run off anytime he moved next to the others. They reached the edge of the kingdom, and they pulled out their air breathers. The breather would turn the oxygen in the water to breathable air for the crew to breathe. They treaded for some time, about forty minutes, until they reached an area with caves all around. The Cap'n was searching for a cave with a man's face next to it, they called this rock the old man of the cave, and he was the first to reach it. He dismounted and announced to the crew, "we be here!" The crew had a hard time hearing him, so he did the next best thing, he pointed at the cave.

The Cap'n pulled out his gun, and Tommy followed in behind him. He quickly turned when he saw a giant creature coming after him, he could tell that it was a Kraken. Tommy hid by the sidewall of the cave. He thought about turning back, but he decided to move forward to find the treasure and hoped the Cap'n and the crew could handle the monster. Tommy was not using a breathing mask, so it was much easier for him to move. Tommy came to an opening in the cave. There was treasure that filled the cabin of the cave. He looked for the stone, but he could not find it. In the back of the cabin, there was a trident on a beautifully designed stand. It looked like it was made just for the trident. On the top, there was a symbol just like in the other cave where they found the *Viola* jewel. He remembered the King's orders, not to forget the trident at all costs. He grabbed the weapon and swam back to the Cap'n.

The Cap'n saw Tommy behind him and aimed his gun at the Kraken. Sarrah quickly pushed his gun down towards the ground. The Cap'n couldn't say too much to the crew. The boys, including Anik, were keeping the Kraken at bay. Joseph and Robert were using their new staffs. Joseph was doing a great job. He was pushing the Kraken back with the currents he made under the water. Robert assumed that he had the same power since he was able to do it too. Tommy was trying to get out of the cave but could not get pass. He was climbing over the mess of tentacles that blocked him. Just then, little Isabel, who was standing behind Joseph, swam towards the Kraken. She could see Tommy was holding the trident. She didn't want Tommy to lose it. She didn't have a plan but was going to distract the monster anyway possible. She reached one of the tentacles of the Kraken and kicked as hard as she could. The Kraken made an awful sound. She swam as fast as she could to Joseph, but she could not reach him in time. The Kraken pulled up its tentacle and swung it at Isabel. She screamed in terror. The tentacle swung right through her. She had turned into a ghost, just like Tommy. Joseph reached the Kraken and slammed it with the largest current he had ever released. It pushed the Kraken far enough for them to mount the seahorses.

The Cap'n was the last to leave with Tommy. Sarrah and Isabel were in front, as Anik was leading the way. Joseph and Robert were both on each side of the Cap'n, continually pushing the Kraken back with their staffs. Martin, who was following the girls, decided now was the best time to see why the horse wanted to be in front. He nudged the seahorse, and they all started to move faster. He moved alongside Anik, and the horses followed them. They were all moving faster than they had before. Anik was surprised that Martin had gotten the hang of the horse so quickly. They were now at a pace that the Kraken had a hard time keeping up with. The Kraken stopped when they reached the outer wall of the kingdom.

They made it back to the stables where Bahrk was waiting. He was very happy to see them. He whimpered and barked a little as he spun with joy. The crew started talking, but a loud cry screeched out. "Isabel," Sarrah shrieked! "What is the matter mommy," Isabel asked? "You are a ghost," Sarrah said. "I'm just like Tommy. Tommy, Tommy, we are the same," Isabel told him. "What happened," Tommy asked in amazement? Anik cleared his throat and pointed to his neck. "What… this," Isabel said as she pulled off the locket that Anik gave her? She turned back to normal. Tommy looked at it. "It's my locket, Isabel," Tommy stated in surprise. "Your locket," Isabel asked? Isabel handed it to him, and he opened it up. There were Tommy and his sister on one side, and his parents on the other. "See," he said. "Tommy, I didn't know. I am so sorry," Isabel cried. Tommy looked at her and thought it was best to give it back to her. "It's yours now. Keep it safe for me." Isabel was so excited that she jumped at Tommy and gave him a huge hug. "Thank you, Tommy," she exclaimed! Anik announced to the crew, "I think the King and I have a few things to explain to you all. I will walk you back to the throne room."

They walked into the throne room. In the King's chair, was the cloaked man from the alley. "So, you are back. Do you have the trident," asked the man? "We are not giving it to you," Joseph said. "I wouldn't expect you to give it to just anyone." The man stood up, and while he was talking, his voice started to sound familiar. He unveiled his cloak, and it was the King.

Sarrah shouted at him, "I thought you said don't hurt your pet! What type of pet is that?" "It's just a baby," the King said. The crew jumped back. The King held out his hand towards Tommy. "I'm sorry, I could not find the *Ocean Sapphire*," Tommy said to the King, as he handed the trident over. "Tommy, you did find it," Bashiri said. He reached to the top of the trident. In the middle of the forks was the symbol again. He slid the latch of the trident open, and the *Ocean Sapphire* popped out. "This, I believe, is yours," he said. "Everything worked out," a man said out from the back. The old man came hobbling into the room. He started aging younger as he got closer to Bashiri. They notice he was wearing Anik's outfit. "Anik, ye be the old man," the Cap'n cried. "Do ye happen to have any more maps," he then asked. "Sadly, not at this time," Anik said. "Why all of this," Sarrah asked? "It was a test to see if you are worthy of the gems. I have been impressed by Tommy, not once but twice for offering the locket to his new family. The Cap'n for taking on such a family, and over the years, he has never succeeded to astonish every time I meet him," Anik revealed. "Now that you have what you were looking for, and I have my trident back, it's time for a celebration. I also believe a little girl wanted to play with the royal kids or so I heard," the King said. Malikah, who had been sitting at her throne the whole time, spoke up, "I think we will have that talk now. Bring Isabel with us, please." "Where ye be goin'," the Cap'n asked while the girls walked out with a handful of maidens? "Going to freshen up," Malikah commanded. "I think its best if we wait but, in the meantime, we can enjoy some music," Bashiri said.

A band started playing in the ballroom; *"It's going down, I'm yelling timber You better move, you better dance Let's make a night, you won't remember I'll be the one, you won't forget."* The Cap'n looked over at **Bashiri**, "tell me one thing I can't understand, how ye knew of the latch and the amulet." "Ha-ha, that was our first ship we built of that model. It was our flagship," Bashiri said. "Wasn't that a good buy I told you about," Anik said. "Arrrrrr, what do ye want from me," the Cap'n said. "The compass," they both said together. "I already promised it to another once I am done with it," the Cap'n said with a grin. "We know, we look forward to doing business with you again," Bashiri said.

The music stopped, and a new band came on the stage. "Shark! Shark!" People were coming out with paper shark heads over their heads. Tommy and Isabel were running around the ballroom as the sharks chased the kids while the song was playing. "We must be goin' now," said Cap'n Samm to both men. "Please stay awhile as we upgrade your ship," Bashiri said. "Upgrade," the Cap'n asked? "Better boosters," Anik said. "What type of boosters? I guess we could stay a day or two, but what ye be talkin' about," the Cap'n asked? "Boosters that work under the water and by sea," Anik said. "That would cost me more than I could afford," said the Cap'n. The King revealed his plan to the Cap'n. "We would hate to see our old flagship not have the absolute best. It may not be my flagship anymore, but it is in good hands. We are in business with you now right, and it has sentimental value to me. Give us forty-eight hours," Bashiri said. "Yes sir," the Cap'n said excitedly.

Chapter 6

Piece 3

The Box

The kids said their goodbyes, and the crew boarded their ship. Tommy and Isabel took to the royal kids well. They enjoyed the time spent at the palace. In the future, they hoped they would be back to play with the kids again. "Set sail," the Cap'n commanded! The crew worked the ship and brought it to the opening of the kingdom. "You ready for this," Martin called to them? "Yeah," they all yelled! "Let's head out," yelled the Cap'n! The Cap'n walked over to Martin, "I will be in me quarters trackin' the next jewel." "Aye, aye sir," Martin replied!

Days passed at sea, about a week and a half, Tommy was looking at the box the Oracle had given him. Isabel was playing ball with Bahrk. Bahrk grew tired of playing ball and went to lay by Tommy. Isabel decided to follow. "Tommy, whatcha up to," Isabel asked? "I'm trying to figure out what's in the box," Tommy said in a monotone voice. "Why don't you just try opening it," Isabel said delightedly? "I don't have a key," Tommy said. "I see, Robert and daddy are always trying to pry treasure open all the time with a crowbar. They get really excited, and then there is a bunch of cracking noise," she carried on. I think that's the wood splitting," Tommy said to her. "Really," she said. "A crowbar is too big," he said. "I see Robert using a screwdriver sometimes," she exclaimed. "Yeah, that will work. Let's go get one from Robert," he remarked.

They ran to Robert. They started to talk to him while he was working on the pumps again. "Robert," Tommy started to say, but Isabel cut him off. "Hi Robert, whatcha doing?" Robert was hard at work, scraping the inners of the bad pump. "Why do you work so hard on the pumps all the time," Tommy asked? "Tommy, if the ship catches fire or if the ship has a hole in it, what are the first things we need" Robert questioned? "The pumps," Isabel shouted! Robert pointed to her and said, "that's right, Isabel. The first thing I'm going to grab is the pumps. That was very good Isabel." Tommy was still looking at him puzzled. "Oh, but why do you fix them all the time," Tommy asked again? "Tommy, they have to work. If they don't work, then I can't use them," Robert stated. "I know that, can I borrow a screwdriver," Tommy asked as he proposed a new question into the conversation. Tommy replied, "to pry open a box." Robert looked at him, "hmm, ok, here. I need it back when you are done." Isabel quickly grabbed the screwdriver, "will do." "Not you and don't run," Robert said to her. She was about to run, but Robert stopped her. "Walk Isabel! That is a tool, and what are tools?" "Tools are dangerous. I remember everything that you tell me!" She had a good memory for a kid, and Robert knew that. Tommy was about to walk out of the room, and Robert stopped him. Isabel was leading the way, when she too stopped at the doorway. "Tommy, what was your question?" "Well, why don't you buy new ones? I'm sure Oscar could find you some good ones." Robert dropped what he was doing and looked at him in shock. Not only did Tommy tell Robert that he could probably buy new ones but also, he can get magical ones. "Tommy! You're a genius. I have to talk to the Cap'n right now! I'll walk with you," Robert bellowed.

They reached the box again, still sitting in the same spot. "Here you go Tommy," Isabel said. "Why don't you go first," Tommy suggested. "You heard Robert, not me, which leaves you or Bahrk." They looked at Bahrk comfortably laying down, looking at them. "Ok, I'll stick the screwdriver in the hole." He put the screwdriver up into the hole, and he got zapped. "Ouch! That hurts," Tommy started to well up. Isabel reacted to him and tried to comfort him.

Meanwhile, by the helm, Robert was talking to the Cap'n. "Cap'n, can I buy new pumps," Robert asked? "What for, the old ones are working just fine," the Cap'n said. "No, they are not. I am constantly fixing them," Robert said. "Ye have? They work like new every time," the Cap'n stated proudly. "Yeah, but I thought you could talk to your new friend, Oscar. You know the one that finds magical objects," Robert was waiting for the Cap'n to take the bait. "We could ask him if he has somethin'. It could cost a fortune," the Cap'n muttered to himself, trying to think it out. "This is to keep the compass from getting lost, and I bet you get a discount for being a business partner," Robert said to him knowing he will mutter to himself for days. The Cap'n jumped up, "that's great thinking there boy. I'll send for him at the next island." Robert was pleased, and he had Tommy to thank for it.

Just then, both kids started crying. Isabel shouted at the box, "let's smash it." "What is goin' on," the Cap'n shouted? "They are trying to open a box," Robert reported to him.

"Stop," the Cap'n shouted! Tommy was holding the box as high as he could. "Tommee, put down the box gently lad. Don't do anything drastic." Tommy looked at the Cap'n and slowly put down the box on the deck. "Tommee, that is a magical box that could be very dangerous," the Cap'n said as he walked over to them. "That box will protect itself no matter what. Fer example, if ye kick that box, it will hurt yer foot, watch," the Cap'n grabbed his sword. Martin called to the Cap'n, "don't do it!" "Sorry, but they have to know." He lifted his sword and gave a quarter of his strength and struck the box. "Whoa," the Cap'n shouted as he fell back in the air and landed on his back. "Ye should treat magic like a tool," the Cap'n said as he was brushing himself off. "Treat it like ye dog," he continued. "So, magic is a tool," Isabel said. "Yes me little ones," the Cap'n limped back to Robert to continue his conversation. He had to ask Robert what he needed in a pump.

"So, what would have happened if Tommy threw that box at the deck," Robert asked? "It would have blown a hole in me ship," the Cap'n exclaimed half in pain. Martin chimed in, "you could have given it less power." Martin looked at him. "I guess I don't know me own strength," the Cap'n replied.

The Viridis Tropics

They made it to the island a day after the incident with the box. Martin docked the ship at the docks. "Ahoy Cap'n," Cap'n Gray called to him. The Cap'n waited for him to come on board. "Cap'n D.W. what…" Cap'n Samm began.

"Shhee, don't call me that name," Cap'n D.W. said. "What might ye be callin' ye-self nowadays," Cap'n Samm asked? "Cap'n Gray," Cap'n D.W. said proudly. "And ye ship? And Huck," Cap'n Samm asked? "The *Gray Wolf* and I just call Huck a mutt," Cap'n Gray replied. "Oh, I see. So, what do we owe the pleasure," Cap'n Samm questioned? "I have brought you a gift. The swords you asked for, courtesy of Oscar," Cap'n Gray said. "I don't believe that. Ye are workin' for Oscar and ye tellin' me that he had someone deliver the swords to me," Cap'n Samm exclaimed! "That's why he told me it was a courtesy, huh," Cap'n Gray said. "Courtesy ye say, well alright then, Martin come on over," Cap'n Samm shouted. Martin walked over to the two captains. "Yes Cap'n," he said. "Why don't ye give this sword a try," Cap'n Samm suggested? Martin looked at him in amazement. Martin unsheathed the left sword. "This feels light, how come?" "It seems that the swords have picked ye. These be fer ye. They come in a pair," Cap'n Samm stated. Martin sheathed the sword again and grabbed both swords. He walked towards the crew who was watching them and started to show the swords to them.

"Cap'n, I must be going. I have much work to do," Cap'n Gray said. "Just a few questions fer ye. How did ye know where I was," Cap'n Samm asked? "Oscar told me," Cap'n Gray said. "But how did he know where I was goin'," Cap'n Samm question? "I don't know. I should probably ask," Cap'n Gray replied. "Would ye mind, and could ye hand him this letter," Cap'n Samm asked I would get rid of this word as it seems that he is asking again but I don't see that he does? "Isabel would ye mind fetching the letter in me cabin," Cap'n Samm called to her. "Yes daddy, right away," Isabel shouted back to him. It took her only a few moments for her to bring the Cap'n the letter addressed to Oscar. "Here ye are," said Cap'n Samm. "I will be on my way then," Cap'n Gray said.

The crew unloaded off the ship and headed towards the market on the island. They stayed close to the Cap'n but was about a stand or two away. The market consisted of stands selling all kinds of goods, and foods that were grown, collected, or made on the island. The Cap'n walked to the fruit stand and started talking to the merchant who was a young woman in her 20's. "Do these cure scurvy," he asked her? "They do," she said to him. "Good, I will be back for these later," he told her. "All of them," she questioned? "Three times as many, if you have them," he said to her. "It will take me some time to procure that many." "We will be here for a few days. Ye may load them onto the ship if ye don't mind," he said. "That one," she pointed to the ship they got off? Yes, the *Night Drifter*," he said. "It will be done," she replied. The Cap'n gave her five gold coins. "That is too much," she said to him. "Then, maybe ye can stock me ship for me with the of the money," he asked her? "That I can do. You will have a stocked ship when you come back," she smiled at him as she said it. He walked over to Sarrah, Tommy, and Isabel. "Ye have the rest of the day me dear," he said to Sarrah. "Good, then you can come shopping with us," she replied to him.

By nightfall, they sat down outside at a tavern. The band was singing, *"when the sun goes down, we start a fire. Start a fire."* They were sitting at some picnic tables that were outside, appreciating the food and the band. "By dawn we will head out, but let us enjoy the rest of the night," the Cap'n said to them.

The Temple

In the morning, they headed for the inner island. The crew came to a clearing outside the village. "Now then, we be lookin' fer a trail," the Cap'n said to them. "I guess we are looking for a big opening," Martin asked? "I assume so," the Cap'n replied. "Are there stones near it," Isabel asked? "Maybe," the Cap'n said. "Are there torches near the entrance," Sarrah asked him? "I don't think there would be torches, it would burn down the whole forest," the Cap'n replied to her. "Would it look scary," Tommy asked him? "It may," the Cap'n said as Robert and Joseph walked closer to the kids and Sarrah. Bahrk was sniffing at the rocks that Isabel pointed out. "Now, the entrance must be around here somewhere," the Cap'n was walking in the opposite direction from them. "Cap'n, can you show me what this is," Tommy asked him. The Cap'n looked up at Tommy and walked over their way. He reached most of the crew and looked down a small trail. The jungle was dense, and vines were hanging down from the trees. The path had been compacted from people walking on it. "This could be it," the Cap'n said to them. "Martin! Martin! Ye be in the back." Martin came jogging towards them. "Aye, aye Cap'n," Martin said. "Now who wants to go first," the Cap'n asked while he was looking at Sarrah? "Yeah, right, you first. If you think I am going first, you're barking up the wrong tree," she replied to him.

Bahrk jumped up at her. "Not you," she said. "Right, me first," the Cap'n said while he pulled out his gun.

They walked for a bit, constantly looking out for danger around every tree or stone. Soon the path opened wider. After a while, the Cap'n opened the compass and looked to see where they were on the map. They then continued for some time.

By midday, they came to a fork in the trail. The Cap'n led them to the left path, and they went down another path. They came to four temples. There was one medium size on the left, and two small ones on the right. In the middle, by the far back, stood a giant temple. They were cautious about approaching the temples. The Cap'n could not sense any danger. "Be careful and don't go in any of the temples," the Cap'n instructed them.

They started to investigate the temples. The Cap'n and Martin were busy making torches. They found branches that were about the size they needed. The Cap'n wrapped the branch, and Martin would douse it with a liquid. They made four torches. Joseph was standing with Tommy and Bahrk at the first of the right temples. Joseph was interested in what was in them. The Cap'n walked up to him, lit a torch, and handed it to him. Joseph poked the torch in and then started to walk in. The Cap'n followed him in, and the amulet around his neck began to glow. Inside they could see square holes cut into the walls. Joseph stepped on a stone that pushed into the ground. The Cap'n heard the clicking. "Joseph," Cap'n Samm yelled as he pulled Joseph! A bunch of arrows shot out of the wall. The Cap'n pulled Joseph towards him, just out of the path of the first holes. "Ok, new plan," the Cap'n said to him. He pulled Joseph out of the temple as he walked towards the center of the area.

"Come here ye all," the Cap'n ordered them. "We don't walk into the temples. They be booby-trapped. Now the question is, how do we find out where the treasure is," he said to them. "Cap'n, what about your compass? Where does it point," Tommy asked? "That's a good question Tommee, where does this compass point to," the Cap'n took out his compass, and it pointed towards the big temple. "It looks like the big one," the Cap'n said to them. "Then, we should only go in that one," Sarrah said. "There must be a point in the three smaller temples. Roll stones in each one of them," Cap'n Samm suggested. They walked up to the temple on the right in the back. They all grab stones and waited for the Cap'n to give them the next command. Tommy was the closest one to him.

"Can I have that lad," the Cap'n asked him? Tommy handed a stone to him. He rolled the stone while Martin held a torch in the room. The Cap'n rolled the stone on the ground, but nothing happened. "Next," the Cap'n said. Isabel walked up to him and handed him a stone almost as big as Tommy's. "Thank you me dear," he said to her as he started to roll that rock down the floor of the temple. The rock hit another switch. The middle of the floor dropped out. "Another please," the Cap'n requested. Sarrah handed the Cap'n another stone. He threw it as hard as he could, and it rolled off into the pit. They could hear snakes hissing at the stone as it landed on the ground. "I hate snakes," Sarrah shouted! "It looks like ye will not be going into that pit anytime soon," the Cap'n said to her. "Very funny," Sarrah replied.

"Ok, onto the next temple," the Cap'n instructed. They moved to the temple on the left. It was a bit bigger than the others. He rolled the first rock, and it hit a trap right away. The walls started to move, and they could see the spikes getting closer and closer to the center of the room. "Stand back," the Cap'n said as the room ended with the walls closing the gap. Apparently, every spike fit perfectly into the walls. "Let's look at the big temple now," the Cap'n walked in first. There he could see a tray on the wall that the other temples did not have. "Hand me a torch," the Cap'n said. Martin walked in careful not to walk past the safe platform. Martin handed him the torch, and the Cap'n put the flame into the left tray. The left side of the room lit with fire going down the tray. He then walked to the right side and again lit the tray. "Right, so don't go beyond the first holes in the wall," the Cap'n said. He was still looking at the entrance of the temple.

They walked in, and Tommy notice that he and Isabel were shorter than the holes. Tommy stopped Bahrk from getting any closer. "Stay boy," he said to him. "Now, how do we get to the other side without settin' off these traps? It seems that the three temples mimic this temple. The traps look to be in a counterclockwise order. See the holes here, those be the arrow holes, and the spikes be in the back," the Cap'n said to them. "If we roll some more rocks, we will know where the traps are," Sarrah stated. "Arrrrrr, but then it will set them off, and the second and third may go off, and that will block us out," the Cap'n said. Tommy walked under the first trap while they were talking. He wanted to see if he could do it. He got about halfway through the first one when Bahrk started to follow. Bahrk mistakenly stepped on a tile, and there were shots of arrows coming out. Tommy hunched over a little while they were shooting. The crew looked out at what was going on. "Tommee, what are ye doin' out there," yelled the Cap'n? "I wanted to see if I could do it! I'm shorter than the holes." "Aye, but these are magical arrows boy. We don't know what they can do to ye," the Cap'n said. Tommy was crawling closer towards the center. Bahrk, who had no reason to craw, was crawling on the ground, mimicking Tommy's moves. "Tommy, you, you be careful, you understand me," Sarrah yelled to him. Joseph yelled to him, "talunt Tommy, I'll back you up!" Tommy and Bahrk made it three-quarters of the way out when the third trap set off. It was the spiked wall, and it started to close.

"Run Tommy," the crew screamed! Tommy and Bahrk got up and started running. Bahrk, who was behind him, set off the trap in the middle. The floor dropped out. Tommy felt the floor drop and jumped as high as he could. He was about halfway in the trap when the double doors opened. Tommy flew further than any of the crew could jump, and just made it to the other side. Bahrk had to stop and started crying when he reached the opening. Tommy ran past the spiked walls that were about halfway closed by this point. "What do I do now Cap'n, I made it," Tommy yelled to him? "Look for a way to undo it. Maybe like a lever," the Cap'n said as the wall closed. "Right a liver, where do I find a liver," he said to himself? Tommy looked around, and on the right side of the room, he could see an hourglass with the sand at the bottom. It looked like the symbol from the caves. Next to it was a lever. He tried to pull down on it, but it would not move. The hourglass spun around in a circle until the sand was at the top. He was surprised that it moved but quickly realized that this was magic. Soon, he became very frustrated at the sand going down as it was taking a long time. As mad as he could get, he pulled with all his might at the lever again, and it quickly pulled down. The wall started to open. It was open enough for him to talk to the Cap'n again. "I did it. I found the liver," he shouted to the Cap'n. "It's a lever son! Oh, never mind, I will explain it to him later," the Cap'n said to the crew, "check the tiles." The crew rolled rocks across the floor, and no arrows went off. Tommy started to look at the room where he found a pedestal with the jewel, the *Emerald of Nature*, which he quickly stuffed into his pocket. He also found another piece of the Treasures of Many, which he grabbed.

By this time, the floor was almost in place, and a side door opened. Tommy caught a glimpse of a person coming out with a big axe that swung at him. He jumped out of the way right away. Tommy shouted at the top of his lungs. "Help!" Bahrk heard this, and he growled. He came charging in and bit the man on his arm. He then grabbed his cloak and pulled him away from Tommy. Also, at this time, the Cap'n heard Tommy, and the crew started running in. The Cap'n was leading the charge directly behind him was Martin. The Cap'n stopped the next swing. "Ye, don't touch me boy," he said to the assailant. "I kill whoever I want," the man shouted. The Cap'n pushed the axe away with his sword as Martin was fighting him off. "Cap'n push him back into the hole he came out of," Tommy said to him. Martin heard and lined him up. The Cap'n took over fighting as Martin backed away. "Now," the Cap'n commanded, and Martin kicked him in. Tommy and the Cap'n closed the slab of thick stone. Martin saw a statue next to the door and pushed it in front of the door. "That won't hold him fer long! Let's get out of here," the Cap'n instructed.

Sarrah, Isabel, Robert, and Joseph were waiting by the entrance. The Cap'n yelled to them, "run back to the ship, and don't stop until ye get there!" He led the way out of the maze. By this time, the crew was tired of running, and they had just made it to the second fork. "Samm, the kids can't run anymore," Sarrah shouted to him! They stopped in the path. "We have to go, we cannot stay long, catch ye breath, and then we continue to run." "Why? No one is following us," Sarrah said to him? "That axe be the *Narflux Axe*, which means that be Narflux and we both have heard the stories of Narflux. So ye see why we have to go," the Cap'n said to them. "Right, catch your breath as fast as you can," Sarrah said. "Mommy, mommy, I can't run anymore," Isabel said. "I'll carry you on my back," Sarrah said. "We will help," the three older boys said at once.

"Tommy, why aren't you out of breath," Martin asked him? "You run next to Isabel, ok? Look after her if she is put down. Got it?" "Ok," Tommy said to Martin. "Joseph what does talunt mean," Tommy asked to Joseph. "Tommy remember talunt, it means, you do what you do," Joseph said. They reached the ship after a few quick breaks. The Cap'n boarded the ship, and the lady from the market was waiting for them. "We must set sail, is everything loaded," the Cap'n asked? "Just finished," she said. "Good. Set sail," the Cap'n commanded his crew. "Aren't you going to stay for a while longer, you just got here," she asked him? "No ma'am. We best be takin' off and fast. We ran into Narflux," he said to her. "We will create a distraction if needed," she said. "Thank ye, take this," the Cap'n handed her ten more gold coins. "This is for your troubles. We be leavin'." She walked off the ship, and the ship started to move away from the port. "Cap'n I found another piece of the book," Tommy said. He was trying to hand it to him. "Go put it in me quarters. I will look at it later," the Cap'n told him. "Warpfrom the pier," the Cap'n instructed. They started their journey off at sea again.

Chapter 7

Piece 4

Sky Island

They were on their way. The trip had lasted three and a half weeks already. Where they were going, they did not know. They were solely relying on the compass to tell them where to go next. Fortunately, they had not seen Narflux since they left the four temples on *Viridis Tropics*. Martin was worried because the compass seemed different again. It was slightly pointing up. It was morning, and Martin had been up all night watching the stars and trying to map where they were. He had to guess that he was further south than he had expected. Martin had just checked the compass, and as he suspected it was now pointing further up and again, it had just turned. Just as the Cap'n commanded last time, he turned the ship and circled the area. The crew came up to the deck. They wanted to know about the sudden shift in navigation.

"Now, what's this all about," asked the Cap'n? "I think we are at our next destination sir," Martin said. "Slow the ship down and go to where it just turns." Martin did as the Cap'n said, and the crew closed up the sails. "Let's see, if I was the *Sapphire of Truth,* where would I be hiding?" It was a cloudy day, and the sun would come out and play but then go hiding again behind the clouds. "Where is it pointing this time," Sarrah asked? "It points upwards," Martin said. They were looking up but did not see anything. Robert suggested to the Cap'n, "maybe the treasure was on a ship that sunk." "No, then it would be pointin' down like the last time," the Cap'n said. "Well, maybe a bird ate the *Sapphire of Truth,*" Sarrah suggested. The crew looked at her and did not say anything. "What, it could happen, I think," she continued. "Maybe the treasure is on a floating island," Tommy said. "Nah, there's nothing up there," the boys said together. "Nothing but clouds," Joseph added. Sarrah and Isabel were looking up in the sky, high above them. Sarrah said, "boys!" They stopped talking, and all three of them looked up too. "How do we get up there," Robert asked? "Get up where me lad? We should be right on top of the treasure now," the Cap'n said, while he was deep in thought. He did not see the crew looking up because he was near the helm, and they were all standing behind him. "Cap'n, Cap'n," Tommy was trying to get his attention. The crew called to him all at once, "Cap'n!" "What is it," the Cap'n was frustrated because the crew broke his concentration, he thought he was on to something. "Look up," Sarrah exclaimed! "What is that and how the blazes do we get up there," he hollered when he saw the floating island? By this point, they have drifted just far enough for it to be behind the *Night Drifter*.

"So, what do you think," Sarrah asked him? The Cap'n pulled out his spyglass. From the ship, he could see a watchtower with a few guards on it. "There be a few guards up there," the Cap'n said to the crew. "Maybe we can get their attention by yelling as loud as we can," Isabel suggested. "No, I have a better idea," the Cap'n said to her as he pulled out his gun. He pointed it at the guard tower and shot. Bang! The bullet hit the shield hanging behind the guards. Just then, a siren sounded off.

"What now? They will think we are shooting at them," Sarrah yelled at him! "Don't ye worry. I'm sure they will look before they shoot, but I suggest ye all sit down, so they don't think we are invaders," the Cap'n said to them. "And what about you, why aren't you sitting," Sarrah asked him? "Me dear, the Cap'n never stands down and may be the first one to go down in a situation like this. So, if that happens, ye will want to run as fast as ye can," the Cap'n replied.

Sarrah looked at him in astonishment that he would take that type of risk. She was also a little infatuated with him though she wouldn't tell him. Sarrah though he was unbelievably brave and handsome. It takes a strong person to do what he just did and she knew it. He posed standing cross-armed facing the island, looking like a true captain with an unwavering resolve. "Yup, the bravest man we know," Robert said to the crew. "Is brave and crazy the same thing,"

Martin asked? They were all laughing and joking as they were waiting.

After a bit of time had passed, they could see something flying towards them. "What is it," Sarrah asked? The Cap'n had his spyglass and was watching a group of young soldiers comprised of both males and females coming towards them. "Prepare ye-selves, they are goin' to board," the Cap'n said. "They? You mean people are flying," Sarrah asked?

They landed in the middle of the ship. The leader of the group spoke first, "why is it you come here, and are you hostile?" "If we were hostile, I would have shot ye before ye made it to the ship. We come for the *Sapphire of Truth*," the Cap'n said to them. "What's that," she replied? The Cap'n nodded to the crew, and they slowly stood up. "It's treasure that we seek," Tommy commented to them. "You have kids here? That is highly unusual for a ship bearing a pirate flag." "We're not ye usual pirates or treasure hunters either. We are looking for powerful magic, magic that is on that island up there," the Cap'n said. "Fine, wait here while we get you up to our kingdom. I'm Cynthia, and you better not make me regret taking you to our queen," Cynthia said. She pulled out a gun and fired it above the island. It made smoke as it shot out and scattered above like a firework. The crew looked at her. "What, it's a flare gun. Have you never seen one before," Cynthia asked? Robert spoke up, "would you be willing to trade for something like that?" "The queen will decide that," she said. "Drop anchor, we be goin' to be a while," the Cap'n commanded.

In about Twenty minutes, a small dragon carrying a small sack in comparison to him landed on the ship. Cynthia untied the sack and started to pull out the items in it. "Let's see. The older boys can have the air boards, the flying saucers for the kids, and the AG boots for the two adults." The older boys strapped themselves onto their boards and put on their gloves. Sarrah and the Cap'n strapped the kids into the flying saucers and put on the boots. "How do they work," Martin asked? "Open one of your hands all the way and then close it for five seconds, that will activate the boards. To shut them off, hold up your two fingers on both hands for 20 seconds and the same with the boots, like this, watch. Raise your hand above your heart, and it will go up; below will go down."

Cynthia gave a demonstration, and they caught on very quickly. "What about the flying saucers," Sarrah asked? "Oh, they just follow you, hold on to them with a robe. They sync with the gloves," Cynthia continued. "What type of magic is this," Sarrah had to know because she was fascinated by it? "AG magic," one of the teen soldiers said. "AG," asked the Cap'n? "Anti-Gravity magic. Now, we must be off. The queen does not like to wait long. She's kind of impatient, so be warned," Cynthia said.

They all started the AG magic items. The boys were unstable at first but were able to get control fast. They reached the city but kept going right into the queens thrown room. The boys were ecstatic. They had so much fun. "Wow! Can we keep them," Joseph asked? "They are yours if you tell me why you shot at my guards," the Queen said. "Your Highness, I was merely gettin' their attention," the Cap'n said. "You shot at them," she said again. "No, I shot at the shield. This gun shoots straight every time, and they were in no danger provided they didn't move in front of the shield," the Cap'n rebutted. "You could have killed them," she said to him. "They were wearing armor. It was a slight possibility, but it worked," he continued. "I see, don't do it again! I am Ayla, my name means *halo of light around the moon*, and this is my kingdom, *Sky Island*. Why are you here," Ayla asked? "We be searchin' fer the *Sapphire of Truth*," the Cap'n said.

"This item," Ayla walked over to a small cabinet and pulled out the gem. It was the *Sapphire of Truth*. "So, ye already saved us the trouble of findin' it. Is there a way of convincin' ye to give it to us," the Cap'n asked? "There is, you can get my bow and arrows back from my dragon," Ayla replied. "We're hardly equipped to fight off dragons, ye Highness," the Cap'n said. "Good, you won't be fighting him. Go to his cave and get the bow and arrows but do not kill him," she said. "Maimin' him is out of the question too, huh," the Cap'n asked? "No hurting him," Ayla told him in a firm voice. "Alright, we are off," the Cap'n said. "We are going to stay here thank you, as I did not sign up to hunt fire breathing dragons," Sarrah said. "Well, that's ye loss. I bet we are goin' to have a great story to tell if we make it out alive, that is," the Cap'n replied.

"Let's go boys," the Cap'n commanded. "I will keep Bahrk and Isabel. I'm guessing Tommy will go with you no matter what I say," Sarrah said. "Tommy, is that the ghost boy's name," Ayla asked? "Yes ma'am." "You cannot go on a flying saucer. You may fall off. Get me a ring of AG," Ayla said. A servant went off, and in a few minutes she returned. "Here, try this on," she said. "It doesn't fit, it's too big,"

Tommy said. Ayla stopped to think. She came up with an idea, fast. "Put it on a chain. It should still work," Ayla said. The servant did as she asked. He put the ring on the chain then tied it onto Tommy's neck. He slowly started to float off the ground. It wasn't too much at first, but then he thought he just wanted to try and go higher, and he reached the extremely high ceiling. "Tommy, how did you do that," Isabel asked?

Isabel had been in awe of the queen, who was young and beautiful with blonde hair and in a white dress. Now her attention went to Tommy, who was always doing amazing things or getting himself in some trouble. She shuttered at the thought of the *Narflux Ax* again. She didn't get to see the axe, but she knew if daddy was running away from it, it was scary. "Mommy, can we talk with the pretty queen," she asked? Sarrah was about to speak up when the queen cut her off. "That would be most delightful. I would love to hear about your other adventures," Ayla said. The servant leaned over to Sarrah. "She likes adventures and kids," she said. "I guess we talk to the queen," Sarrah said. "Tommee, come down here boy, we got to go," the Cap'n said. Tommy came down. He had been exploring the paintings on the ceiling. The rest of the crew and Cynthia's guards went out.

Dragon Tag

The crew followed Cynthia, who was within eyesight of a dormant volcano. There was a cave about a half-mile away. "I suggest we wait to see if he leaves. Cynthia, we should go to that other smaller volcano and wait," the Cap'n said. "We are off. I'm not foolish enough to go up against that dragon." And with that, they took off. The Cap'n shouted at them, "thanks fer ye help!" "What do we do now," Martin asked? "We wait until he leaves," the Cap'n said. "How do you know he is in there," Joseph asked? "Do ye see the smoke comin' out of the cave? That's the dragon's fire," he said.

Some time passed, and they saw the dragon leave the cave and move off the island, it was about mid-day. "Now boys, let's go," the Cap'n said. The Cap'n and Tommy were the first into the cave while the rest stood guard watching for the dragon. Martin couldn't use his swords in fear of dropping them and losing them over the island, so he felt quite vulnerable. Joseph was holding his staff in both hands. Robert was holding his staff in one hand and covering the sun from his eyes while watching for the dragon with the other.

In the cave, they were looking for the bow. "Which bow is it," Tommy questioned, as he knew they had to hurry. "It's the queen's bow, so look for somethin' flashy." Tommy was looking on the right of a giant mound of treasure, while Cap'n Samm was looking on the left. Tommy saw a bow that was sticking out. He started to look on top of the mound where he suspected the dragon laid. "Cap'n, would it be white," Tommy asked? "Does it look suited for a queen," the Cap'n replied? "It has a fancy carving on it," Tommy said. "That's it! Grab the arrows with it." The Cap'n was bent over looking at a bow that he decided to grab and a few gold coins too. He stuffed them into his pocket, and they ran out of the cave. When they came out of the cave, Martin grabbed the bow and arrows from Tommy. "The dragon is on his way," Martin said to them. "Go. Go. Go," the Cap'n said to them.

They were speeding on their way when the dragon came up behind them. They could hear it behind them. They shifted to the left as the dragon took a large gasp of air and then fire bellowed out. Tommy was in front. Robert pushed his staff back in the direction of the dragon. He was hoping to knock the dragon off his course. The dragon made another attempt, but as the dragon opened his mouth, Robert hit him with a burst of air using his new staff. The dragon was caught off guard and pulled back. They did not see how far because the dragon was in the clouds. They made it further to *Sky Island*, but the dragon came back and got close to Martin, who was carrying the bow. Joseph and Robert shot their staffs, but because they were behind the dragon, they couldn't knock him off course.

Just then, Tommy had an idea. He slowed down close to Martin. "Martin, give me the bow," he said. Tommy went next to the Cap'n. "What be the plan boy," the Cap'n asked? The dragon saw the other bow on Cap'n Samm's back. He gave an awful roar. "Spread out," Tommy yelled! Martin and the Cap'n got further away from each other, leaving Tommy in the middle. Robert was following the Cap'n while Joseph was following Martin. The dragon didn't know which one to go after until he saw the bow Tommy was holding.

Tommy stopped when he heard the dragon gasping for air. The dragon slowed down as he blew fire above his head, missing Tommy. The dragon was now behind Robert, and he struck the dragon with another burst of air. Tommy flew back to the Cap'n and Martin. They raced over the streets and houses in town and right into the throne room. The dragon followed them in and landed. He went to blow another fireball when Isabel yelled at him, "you can't touch my daddy!" Ayla stood in front of Isabel, who was in the line of his fire. "Dignity! Stop this instant! I won fair and square," Ayla yelled at him! Dignity, the dragon, was forced to choke back his fire but let out a bellow of smoke. He seemed very displeased at this and laid down at her feet, smoke still coming out of his nostrils. "You can thank me for saving your lives. See, I can have adventures too," Ayla said. They were baffled at what to say but not the Cap'n. "Thank ye, ye Highness. Here be ye bow back." He gestured to Tommy. Tommy walked to the queen and handed her the bow.

Tommy was surprised that the dragon did not move when he got close to Ayla. The dragon puffed smoke at Tommy when he walked away. "Oh, stop. You're just a sore loser," she said to the dragon. "Isabel, are you ok," Sarrah shouted as she hugged her? "Don't worry. She was not in any danger. He won't hurt children. I made sure of that," Ayla said to Sarrah. The dragon nuzzled Isabel. Isabel reminded him of Ayla when she was little. "So, we weren't in any danger," Martin asked her? "Oh no, you're not innocent. You stole the dragon's treasure. You should never do that. They will hunt you down until they get it back. He should have killed you. I have never seen anyone make it this far." The boys jumped back. "Cap'n, you shall have your treasure and the last half of the magical item book." She walked over to the cabinet again and grabbed both. She pushed the book into Cap'n Samm. "Huff," he puffed out.

"Let's have a banquet to honor this occasion." The servants asked the crew to follow. They were going to clean up before dinner. The boys went with the male servants, and the girls followed the women. "Come on boy," Tommy said to Bahrk, he was glad to see him again.

They sat in a great big dining hall. The crew sat at the guest seats, which was close to the queen so that she could hear them. There was food of all types. Plenty of duck, wild boar, and veggies. The violin started to play. It was the most beautiful thing Tommy and Isabel had ever heard. When the music came to an end, Ayla spoke, "we have beds made up for you in the guest-chambers. How would you like to stay?" "I was hopin' ye had a way to transport letters," Cap'n Samm said. "Yes, you may use my dragon mail service. It should only take a few days, depending on where it is going." "The *City of Verdel*," Cap'n Samm said. "Dignity can transport the letter in two days. All though you may have to use another one as Dignity will want to stay with Bahrk and Isabel. He likes little girls, and he's the king of the animals or so he thinks." Ayla looked annoyed at the thought of the dragon being the king of the animals. "Is he king of the other dragons," Tommy asked? "He is that. We had a lot of dragons here at one point. He still wanders in with animals and an occasional dragon," Ayla said. "Are they dead,"

Isabel asked? "Sometimes." Ayla was now thoroughly annoyed at the dragon. "I might just let him steal something else of mine to keep him in his cave, but enough about that, let's hear the next song." The band started playing. *"I'll forgive and forget, before I'm paralyzed. Do I have to keep up the pace? To keep you satisfied."* The band sang.

Once, the band stopped playing, the queen inquired about the crew's next adventure, "where are you going next, Cap'n Samm?" "Not too sure, but we have to find the next gem. However, there be a more urgent matter, we have to find Robert and Joseph's uncle. We've been told he is on *Volcano Island*," he said. "I heard that the *Tangerine Opal* is on *Volcano Island,* though I'm not sure where it could be," Ayla said. "Then, maybe we can hit two birds with one stone," Cap'n Samm said. Ayla got angry at the Cap'n. Don't you dare hit any birds," she said! "No Queen, it be a figure of speech. I will not be hittin' any birds anytime soon," the Cap'n laughed.

Dear Oscar,

      We are planning a breakout of Robert and Joseph's uncle. He is located on Volcano Island. I also suspect the *Tangerine Opal* is on the island. I was told this by the Queen Ayla of Sky Island where the dragon came from.

P.S.

      Be careful of this one, he has a tenancy of blowing fire.

Cap'n Samm,

      I assume by the time you get this letter a week will have passed. Please allow for 2 weeks after you get this letter to meet at the Island of Kumica.

P.S.

      The dragon lit my cat on fire. Send a different one next time, maybe one friendlier towards cats. She did not like getting doused in water.

Chapter 8

Piece 5

Island of Kumica

The time had passed since Oscar sent his letter, and they met on the *Island of Kumica*. Oscar was waiting at the docks for the *Night Drifter*. Cap'n Samm walked off the ship to meet him and Cap'n Gray. "I didn't think ye would be comin' in person," Cap'n Samm said. "This is my time to shine. I have brought men for your ship to watch Isabel while you are on the island," Oscar replied. "Oh, I'm not sure if I want to bring her on this trip or the dog," Cap'n Samm said. "I brought my wife, Julia. I suppose they can stay with her while you are on this excursion. Julia, Mr. Assistant, could you watch the dog and little Isabel for them," Oscar asked? "The girl is no problem, however, not the dog, that's all you Mr. Assistant," Julia said. She didn't like calling the butler Mr. Butler, but Oscar didn't mind Mr. Assistant, so the two of them referred to the butler as Mr. Assistant. "My pleasure, ma'am," the assistant said. "Thank ye. Can ye keep the men in the haul in case anyone tries to board me ship while we be on the island," Cap'n Samm asked? "Of course, the ship must stay intact. Cap'n Gray will be watching from a distance in case you need to get out fast," Oscar said.

"Here's the plan. First, we get on the island without raisin' suspicion. I was goin' to use Robert and Joseph as slaves.

Oscar did ye send the island a letter for open trade," Cap'n Samm asked? "Yes, your name is Cap'n Rogers, my very finest slave merchant," Oscar replied. "That will get us on the island. The crew will do the rest. Martin will be waitin' near the ship, ready for a quick getaway. Tommee will have the compass and look fer the *Tangerine Opal*," Cap'n Samm informed them. "Why Tommy, Cap'n Samm," Cap'n Gray asked? "No one will notice a slave child wonderin' about, and he is the only one we have," Cap'n Samm replied. "Does Tommy know," Oscar asked? "He's the one that volunteered for it. The crew has been goin' over the plans since Oscar replied to me letter. Now, we know that Robert and Joseph's uncle is a doctor and looks at the new recruits whenever they come in. My wife will follow the slaves in to look after them, so I don't get stiffed," Cap'n Samm said. "Let's hope it works," Oscar said. "Will ye be goin' with Cap'n Gray," Cap'n Samm asked Oscar? "No, I will be staying on the island as a merchant as well as to look after my wife and the kids. I wish I could go," Oscar said. "We be off. I want to get there by noon," Cap'n Samm said.

"Isabel, come with me, we are going shopping," Julia yelled up to the ship. "Get the dog," she said to the assistant. "Isabel, you stay with Julia for now and be good for her. We will be back soon," Sarrah said to her. "We all have our missions. It's time to move out," Cap'n Samm said. They sailed until noon and made it just as the Cap'n had planned.

The Escape

The *Night Drifter* did not pull into the dock this time, it sat at sea. The crew rowed a skiff to the docks. Tommy hid under a crate cover. "Ahoy," the Cap'n said to the guards. Martin threw the guards the skiff rope. They pulled the skiff in and tied it off. Robert and Joseph where tied in shackles and were relying on Sarrah to get them out when the time came. She was also carrying their staffs, pawning them off as her own.

"I have these slaves for ye," the Cap'n said. They unloaded the skiff. Sarrah held her Scimitar swords behind the two slaves. "Sarrah, see to it that they do not leave ye sight until I come fer ye," the Cap'n announced loud enough for the guards on the shore to hear him. "Yes sir. Move it scum," she said. "Follow us," one of the three guards said. "Cap'n, this way," the last guard said. "I will wait by the skiff, my Cap'n," Martin said. "Very well," the Cap'n replied. The guards led the slaves and Sarrah to the assessment cell. It was inside the cave system to the left. The Cap'n went to the right.

Martin pulled the sheet off Tommy. "Alright Tommy, you know what you have to do, right," Martin asked? "Yes, I do. Don't let anyone see the compass, and act scared and afraid of anyone that gets to close," Tommy said. "Good, here are the shackles for you to blend in. They are not pinned so they can fall off. Now off with you," Martin told him. Tommy had a grain bag over him to hide the compass and to look like a slave child. He could see slaves bringing diamonds out in carts that had to be processed. He walked into the cave entrance. "Hold it, where are you going," a guard asked who was guarding the entrance of the cave? Tommy didn't know what to do. He didn't have to act scared. He was scared, but he remembered the plan the Cap'n gave him. "I'm sorry. I was asked to go into the mine to pick more diamonds. They need me in the small spots," Tommy said. "You there, Fat Orc, find the smallest hole you can and put this slave in it," the guard said. The Orc was furious about this, as Tommy could see. Tommy had to think quickly on his feet. This was not part of the plan. "Thank you, sir. It will be a pleasure to dig your gems out for you." The Orc was surprised at Tommy's words, but there was something off about the boy. "Yes sir," the Orc said. He thought at least he could find a place for Tommy out of sight of the guards. "Follow," the Orc said to Tommy. Tommy did not say anything else, he just followed.

Tommy could hear the slaves singing. *"Listen to the wind blow; watch the sunrise. Running in the shadows, damn your love, damn your lies. And if you don't love me now, you will never love me again. I can still hear you saying. You would never break the chain. Never break the chain."* Tommy really was acting like he was listening to the slaves, but he was trying to figure out how he could get away from the Orc. "I can find my own way from here," Tommy said. "No, got to find you a safe spot away from the guards," the Orc said. Tommy could see slaves walking the cave paths. They came to a fork in the path, and Tommy stopped, pulling out the compass. "I need to go left," Tommy said. "There's nothing there. Who are you? You are not a slave," the Orc said.

Tommy stopped to think of what he should tell him. "I was ordered to go that way," he said. "That shaft has been abandoned for a few years. You are not a slave," the Orc said. "What is your name," Tommy asked? "Baybar," the Orc replied.

Tommy didn't feel that Baybar was a threat to him, so he decided to fill him on the plan. "I'm not a slave. We are here to break out my brothers' uncle. I need to find something that will help us," Tommy confessed. Baybar pulled Tommy into the empty shaft where there was no one near. "Who is their uncle," Baybar asked? "Robert and Joseph's uncles name is Alan Craze," Tommy said. "Doctor Craze," Baybar looked in surprise. They continued to walk as Tommy led the way. He had the captain's lit amulet that the captain handed him while they were on the ship. Baybar carried a torch and said, "I want to help." "I'm not sure how you can help," Tommy confessed.

They stopped at a giant boulder that Tommy could not move. Baybar saw Tommy trying to move the boulder. "Stand aside," Baybar said. He rolled the boulder out of the way. "That's how it's done. I want freedom too," he told Tommy. "The Cap'n told me to say that if I get into trouble to ask people to find Cap'n Rogers. He said to use the words, "I'm looking for the diamond haul. The keywords are diamond haul. Find the Cap'n and say diamond haul to him. He is collecting slave money," Tommy told Baybar. "Find Cap'n Rogers," Baybar repeated as he started to walk off to the command chamber. "Thank you for your help," Tommy replied as he left.

In no time, Baybar made it to the chamber where there were guards at the door. "Need to talk to the Master," he told the guards. "What for," one replied? "The diamond haul is ready. We found a big one this time. One of the largest I have seen," Baybar said. "Go in, but don't say a word until you are spoken to," the guard told him. Baybar walked in and shut the door behind him. The Cap'n and the Master were discussing prices. "Thirty gold is to cheap. Oscar said he wanted no less than sixty fer each slave. These be premium slaves and hold a high value. They be ten years before their prime, the best slaves ye can buy," the Cap'n said to the Master. Baybar was not going to miss his chance with the Cap'n. "Sir," he said. "What is it Orc? I am in the middle of a deal. This better be important," the Master said rather disgusted.

"We found a big diamond in the diamond haul," Baybar said . The Cap'n took notice. "A big one ye say. Sounds like ye have the money to pay fer me slaves," the Cap'n butted in. "That's two weeks in the hole for you Orc," the Master was very irritated by the Orc. "You promised that I could spend a week by the bay," Baybar replied. "You will never see the bay again, you big oaf, be gone," he replied. "No, you promised me six months ago," Baybar said. The Cap'n was sure Tommy had sent the Orc. "Are you disobeying an order," the Master demanded? Cap'n Samm knew where this was going, as he saw the Master lift up his pistol to the giant Orc. The Cap'n had no time to make any other decisions, he pulled out his pistol and shot the Master in the right shoulder. Baybar swung his big arms into the Master sending him flying into a wall rendering him unconscious. He turned to the guard's chest and knocked them into the wall.

"Ye can spend every day at the beach from now on. What is ye name and did Tommee send ye," the Cap'n questioned? "Baybar. Is that the ghost boy's name? He's safe," Baybar said. The doors opened, and the two guards charged into the room. The Cap'n pulled out his swords and began cutting and slashing at the guards. They were to hurt to move and slunk down in front of the doors. "Then what is the trouble, me friend," the Cap'n asked? "I want freedom," Baybar said. "Do the other slaves," the Cap'n asked? "Yes," Baybar replied. "In that case, we have a breakout! Round up as many slaves as ye can and ask them to help out," the Cap'n told Baybar. A few of the other slaves were in the room with them and found weapons wherever they could, breaking chairs and tables and collecting the legs to use as clubs. "Show me where Tommee is," the Cap'n said to Baybar.

Robert and Joseph walked into an inspection cell, it was a big empty room. They were shackled to the floor, and a door was bar the way. Sarrah had followed them, taking notice of the extra two guards outside the cell. "Leave wench," the guard on the right said to her. "Not until the Cap'n reclaims me. I am under strict orders to stay with the slaves," Sarrah said, hoping they would buy it. The guard grinned at her in disgust and said nothing more. Fifteen minutes later, an older slave came into the room. "Let's get on with it now chaps," he said. The boys recognized him right away. He was older but still had all of their uncle's characteristics. Robert gestured to Sarrah. He wanted to talk to his uncle first.

"What's your name," Robert asked him? "Dr. Craze," he replied. "Do you remember me doctor? I saw you before, about six years ago," Robert said. "Is that so, that would be the time I came to the island. What is your name lad," Dr. Craze asked? "That's slave," the first guard said. The doctor inspected Robertlooking him over with deep inspection, he looked over every freckle on his back. "My name is Robert, sir," Robert said. Dr. Craze paused for a moment but did not seem to take any notice. He finished and moved on to the next boy. "And what is your name slave," the Doctor asked Joseph. "Joseph, sir," he replied. "Slaves don't have names," the first guard said as he pulled out his whip. The second guard had not said anything until this point. "It's Dr. Craze, you know he's a little senile," the second guard said. "Thank you, William. That will make the next part even easier for," the Doctor said. "What is the next part," Sarrah asked, knowing it couldn't be right?

"Castrating these nice young men, so they do not have kids. It's a new rule since last month. You can all leave now," the doctor said. "No! My Cap'n told me to stay with the slaves," Sarrah jumped in when she heard this. "You can stay, though it won't be pleasant. The last slave left my ears ringing for days," the doctor said. The guards where to appalled to stay any longer. The guards left the room, letting Sarrah remain with the doctor. "You can put her to work," the first guard said as he closed the doors. The doctor waited until the doors were shut, and it was safe to talk.

"Boys! How did you get here? Oh, I wish these were under better conditions," the doctor stated. He was happy and afraid to see them. "We are here to break you out uncle," Joseph said. "Who is this lady," he asked? "This is Sarrah, she is like our mother, she takes excellent care of us," Robert said. "Bless you young lady," Dr. Craze told her. "Call me Sarrah, but we don't have time for that. We have to get past the four guards," she said. "That is problematic," Dr. Craze said while rubbing his chin. "I was expecting just two guards, not two more at the door," Sarrah announced. "Think I have a way out of this, but getting to the ship will be impossible with," the Doctor was interrupted by the sound of the doors opening. They could hear what sounded like war cries from off into the cave. The first guard stepped in, followed by the second guard. "Kill them all," said the first guard. He reached for his sword and lifted it over his head, ready to strike Dr. Craze. William, the second guard, would not stand for this, as he admires Dr. Craze. The doctor helped him many times with the slaves. The doctor also saved his life once. William reacted without thinking and knocked the first guard out with a swing of his fist.

"I owed you one doctor," William said. He barred the door behind him. "What is going on," the doctor asked? "There has been a slave breakout. I figured I could get you out in the shuffle," William said. "Well, not like that, lose the guard uniform and put on these," the doctor said. "Can we trust him," Joseph asked? "With my life," the doctor replied. "Good enough for us," Sarrah said. William changed just in the nick of time. They heard loud screaming right before the doors opened again. "You're free," a slave said to them. The boys grabbed their staff from Sarrah and led the way out of the caves.

Baybar led the Cap'n to Tommy. "Tommee, ye be in there," the Cap'n shouted into the caves that the boulder was blocking? Tommy came out headfirst. "I have it Cap'n. It was a small space, but I found the *Tangerine Opal* at the end of the tunnel," Tommy said. "Time to go. Hold on to that tightly," the Cap'n replied. The three of them met up with Sarrah's crew, who was waiting for them at the inside of the cave. They all left the cave following the last of the slaves out.

The slaves were fighting against the guards who spent most of their time outside enjoying the sun. The crew began fighting when they were halfway to the skiff, with Joseph on the left and Robert on the right. Sarrah stayed next to Tommy and the doctor, who couldn't fight too well. William was also next to Dr. Craze, fighting off the guards. The guards were outraged when they saw William leaving with the crew. The Cap'n was leading the charge to the shore, where the last of the guards were. He saw Martin running to him. Charging behind Martin was a guard holding an ax. The Cap'n made a quick decision to pull out his pistol and shoot. He shot and it grazed Martin, but took out the guard. "You shot me," Martin exclaimed! "It's just a graze. I can patch you up. It's not bad," the doctor said as he was looking at the wound. "I've been shot, how is that not that bad," Martin questioned.

Baybar and the rest of the slaves took out the last guard and cheered. "It looks like ye will get that wish after all Baybar," the Cap'n said. "Thank you! What shall we call you our heroes," Baybar asked? "The *Night Raiders*," he replied.

"What happened," Sarrah cried? "Well, the slaves wanted their freedom. The slaves outnumbered the guards, twenty to one, so I figured the odds where in our favor," the Cap'n said. "How do you expect to get all the slaves off the island," Sarrah asked? "No, this is our island now. We protect it,"

Baybar said as the slaves cheered. "Best we be goin', I don't think we want to be around when they pass judgment," the Cap'n said. "Why's that," Sarrah asked? They will be sendin' the survivors to the gallows," the Cap'n said. "We will always be indebted to you," Baybar said. "Much obliged, but ye owe us nothin'. We were glad to help," the Cap'n said.

Most of the crew boarded their skiff, and the rest took another skiff. The *Night Drifter* crossed Cap'n Gray's path, and the Cap'n signaled him to follow, but the Gray Wolf did not follow. They reached the Island of Kumica again. It was late night when they arrived. The boys were talking to Dr. Craze, who was thrilled that he was part of this new crew.

Cap'n Samm and Sarrah went to look for Isabel. They found the assistant outside of the inn drinking a cup of tea. "Cap'n, we weren't sure if you were going to make it in tonight," the butler said. "Mr. Assistant, we are here to pick up Isabel and Bahrk," Sarrah said. "Have a drink first. You must be parched from the long journey," he said. "It's alright. I feel I should get Isabel before she outstays her welcome," Sarrah said. "Very well, follow me this way," Mr. Assistant said. He walked them into a room with a large bed where Julia, Isabel, and the baby where sleeping. Oscar was sleeping in a chair at the end of the bed.

The assistant gently woke Oscar and then Julia. "How were they," the Cap'n asked? "Isabel was a doll, however, the dog was a little unruly. He listens to Isabel's every command, though," Julia said as she was waking up. "Isabel didn't give you any trouble," Sarrah asked? "Not at all. She was a perfect little girl for us," Oscar said. "Thank you for watching her. We will be taking her now," Sarrah said. "No! I mean, I want a girl just like her," Julia said. Oscar jumped fully awake. "It seems little Isabel has left quite an impression on my wife. Anyways we rented rooms for all of you," Oscar said. "Can we go shopping tomorrow," Julia asked Sarrah? "Yes, I would love to," Sarrah couldn't pass up a day out with the girls. "That will give me time to say bye to Isabel. We had so much fun today," Julia said. "I have to talk to ye about Volcano Island," the Cap'n said, as he picked up Isabel, who stayed asleep in his arms. "Let's go Bahrk," the Cap'n said. Oscar nudged Bahrk awake, who was sleeping at his feet. "After you, Mr. Assistant," the Cap'n said. The assistant showed them to Isabel, Tommy, and Bahrk's room. The Cap'n laid her in bed and went to get the rest of the crew. Sarrah stayed with Isabel and Bahrk until the crew came in.

Chapter 9

Piece 6

Dark Island

The next morning the crew met Oscar over breakfast. "Isabel let's go shopping with your mommy," Julia said. The three girls went off taking the baby too. "Boys, find ye somethin' to do. I have to talk to Oscar," the Cap'n said. Tommy and Bahrk followed Martin in one direction, while Robert, Joseph, Dr. Craze, and William when to buy clothes and supplies for Dr. Craze and William. "There is an urgent matter to attend to," Oscar said. Oscar, the assistant and the Cap'n went to the bar.

"What's this all about," the Cap'n asked? "Narflux claimed that island, and you just freed it. That was not part of the plan," Oscar said. "The plan changed, nothin' I could do about that," the Cap'n said. "Just so you know, Narflux is part of the gods," the assistant said. "Then I better be on me guard," the Cap'n said. "Narflux is not the type of man we want to go up against. I heard scary stories about him. I have never heard a story of anyone winning against him. If you see him, RUN. I'm sure you are on his hit list by now between the gem he was watching and now Volcano Island," Oscar said. "I'll warn me crew," the Cap'n said. They continued to talk about business and the book of magic items for the remainder of the day.

They had restocked the ship and were ready to set sail. The *Night Drifter* left port and headed out to sea. About a day later, the Cap'n made an announcement. "Crew, we best be on our guard. After the last island, we may be in hot water, but I will not be deterred in findin' the rest of the compass. We have two pieces to go; the *Diamond of Yew* is the next piece we be after. Let's be watchful with this one," the Cap'n said.

They sailed about three weeks, and the sky started to get dark. The mirrors were working ever so slightly due to the moon being so dim in the sky. It was like the darkness was covering them. The Cap'n did not like the feeling. "Martin, be on ye guard. It seems there be a darkness here. Wherever we be goin' it's uncharted territory," Cap'n Samm said.

"Land-ho," Joseph yelled. The crew raced to the deck of the ship. "I don't see anything," Isabel said. "Martin turn the ship one-eighty. If Joseph says there's somethin' there, then we must be close," the Cap'n said. Martin turned the ship. "We're close to running aground," Martin said. When they turned, they could feel the hull lightly scrape up against the seabed. "That was closer than I like to admit," Martin said. "Drop the anchor," the Cap'n commanded. "I think it's just deep enough," Robert said. "Dampen the mirrors to minizieds the lights and extinguish the lights," the Cap'n commanded once again. "Martin, Robert, come with me. The rest stay with the ship," the Cap'n said. "There is no way you are leaving us on a spooky dark ship," Sarrah said to the Cap'n. "This adventure is goin' to be dangerous," the Cap'n said. "We are in this together," Sarrah replied. "Fine, who's comin', say aye," the Cap'n asked? "Aye," most of the crew said. Dr. Craze thought it was best to stay with the ship. Since Dr. Craze didn't say anything, neither did William. "We will stay and watch the ship. You know what they say, hope for the best but plan for the worst. I'll be prepared for anything when you come back," Dr. Craze said.

The crew rowed onto the beach. The Cap'n was the first one off the boat. "We don't know what may be in this forest, so stay close and be on the lookout," the Cap'n said. It was quiet, too quiet. They walked down a path following the compass. They had an eerie feeling that someone was watching them. In the far distance, they could see eyes staring at them. The Cap'n and the crew had their weapons out and ready. They came to a narrow path when they were attacked. Nets dropped down on them, and skeletons with armor, swords, and shields came out. Joseph noticed Tommy could pass through the net. He was in the middle of Joseph and Martin. "Tommy, stop! We can't get out of the nets," Joseph shouted! In a low voice, so the skeletons could not hear he said, "pretend that you are stuck like us. Talk to the Cap'n as soon as you can." "What be the meanin' of this," the Cap'n shouted? From what he could tell, a first sergeant commanded the platoons. "Take them to the camp and lock them up." The skeletons picked up the crew one by one. It was two skeletons per crew member, and they held the nets by a pole. The Cap'n had four carrying him. They carried them on poles with the net wrapped around it.

Tommy played the part and made sure he wouldn't fall out of the net. It was harder than it looked since he really just wanted to run and hide, but he needed to talk to the Cap'n first like Joseph said. He was in the same net as Joseph.

"Joseph, what if there is a magic cage," Tommy asked? "When I say go, go run and hide. Make sure you don't get caught. Go now," Joseph said. Tommy slipped out of the net. Thankfully, he was in the last net with Joseph, and the skeletons didn't notice him. He was harder to see and more invisible than usual. Tommy got to a safe distance where he could see the crew, but the guards could not see him. He waited until the skeletons settled down and left the crew in the cage. He crept slowly up to the cage. He found a spot where he could talk to the crew without being seen. "Cap'n, Cap'n," Tommy said in a low voice. "Tommee, good job gettin' out me lad," Cap'n Samm whispered. "I can get the key," Tommy said. "Negative. I heard them say they be takin' the key to the castle. I need ye to do somethin'. Take the compass. Find the gem. We will make a distraction," the Cap'n said. "At the first sign of trouble, you run and hide," Sarrah told him. Tommy took the compass and ran to the left side of the camp.

Soon he came upon a mound of bones, the largest he had ever seen and quite possibly the only pile of bones he had ever seen. He started to become more invisible as he heard a voice. "Awe, what fresh set of bones do we have this time," a set of bones said. He started to piece together: first, the feet then the legs. The body began to turn into a man. Finally, the skeleton picked up his head and rested it on his shoulders. "Where is my hat? The name's Bones Weary, you can call me Bones," he said. He grabbed his hat off another skeleton. "Larry, you had my hat for all these years," Bones said. "Who are you," Tommy asked? "Why, the names Bones. I thought I mentioned that already. What, ahh! You are NOT a skeleton, my friend," Bones said looking quite puzzled. "No, I am a ghost. Are you going to eat me," Tommy asked?

"No, I don't think I have a blood thirsting lust. Do you," Bones asked? "No. I'm on a mission," Tommy replied. Bones could see him better now. Ghosts don't normally resonate with me, it's usually only other skeletons," Bones replied. "Not a skeleton, just a ghost named Tommy," Tommy replied. "I thought you were a newcomer. I greet all of them and get their story. Although you do have a different type of spirtual signature," Bones said. Tommy opened the compass and started to walk away. "Hey, where are you going," Bones inquired? "I'm on a mission," Tommy replied. "All alone," Bones asked? "Yes. My crew has been taken, but now I got to find the gem for my Cap'n," Tommy stated. "You have a ship, that's great! I can finally get off this Island and begin a new adventure. This place is kind of grim since I woke up. Tell you what, I'm going to help you. I can't leave a kid all alone in this spooky place. Hey guys, do you want to come with me on an adventure," Bones asked? A femur boned hit him in the shin. "Fine! If you don't want to come, you could have just said so," he said. "Are there more of you," Tommy asked? "Oh yeah, there's a pile of us. The whole mound is made up of skeleton bones, but they are a bunch of lazy bones. So how do you know where you are going," Bones asked? "I'm following the compass my captain gave me," Tommy replied.

"How does it work," Bones asked? "It finds magical items," Tommy said. "Is that the *Compass of Ginar*? That's not good. People are looking for it, very powerful people! You will need all the help you can get," Bones said. "How do you know people are looking for it?" "Oh, I heard it through the grapevine, see." Bones walked to a grapevine and pulled it up to his ear. "Yup, the grapevine is very chatty today," Bones said as he held it up to Tommy's ear. Tommy could hear all sorts of chatter coming from it. "I see. I don't gossip that much, though," Tommy said. "Grapevines are not for everyone," Bones said. They walked a while, and Bones noticed something. It was white and round. Bones could make out what it was the closer it got.

"Tommy, that's a Prison Sentinel. Quick, hide behind that big tree," Bones exclaimed. He was panicking and hyperventilating. The Sentinel grew closer to Bones. It looked like a giant eyeball with four tentacles on both sides. Bones moved in front of Tommy, who was behind the tree. The Sentinel made an awful shrieked at Bones with all eight tentacles that had razor-sharp teeth on them. Tommy felt sick. He noticed he was becoming more invisible again. He wondered if this was working to his advantage. "Hi! How do you do? Nice day. It's dark and gloomy just the way you like it, right? Do you remember if it was always this dark, I mean the last time I rested my bones here it was a really nice place? I guess the real estate has gone down. I mean, when was the last time it was day," Bones frantically said? The Prison Sentinel shrieked at him and then turned right, and continued moving. Bones waited until he couldn't see it anymore. "Tommy, that's not good. Prison Sentinels never come this far out. Do you think they are looking for you?" "I don't know, but I must keep moving, my family is counting on me," Tommy said.

"Oh, you have a family. I forgot what that was like," Bones said as he lowered his head. "My crew is my family. They are not my real mother and father, but I consider them to be like my mother and father," Tommy said. "Oh, you are adopted," Bones stated. "I've made many friends, and I think of them as my family. If I can't have my blood family, then I'll choose my own," Tommy said proud of himself. Oh, I get it, your friends are your family. Tommy, I'm going to have the largest family I can in that case. I'm going to make so many friends. I'll skip the mom and dad thing. I think I'm a little too old for that, but I'm going to have the most brothers and sisters I can. I always wanted brothers and sisters," Bones exclaimed. "Well, what about Larry," Tommy asked? "Yeah, I got Larry, that's a start. Although I don't think he will like me calling him brother. He doesn't like his brothers. As a matter of fact, he doesn't like anything. I wonder when he will come out of his sleep. He's always grumpy when he's taking a nap," Bones said.

While they were talking, Tommy was following the compass north. He felt best staying away from the camp and unknown danger. He figured the compass was pointing northeast, so if he just went north, the compass would turn east at some point. He wasn't expecting company. However, he was enjoying it and was comforted by Bones' excitement in life. They were starting to climb uphill when they heard a low hiss. It popped out behind them. "Tommy, it's a giant spider! I hate spiders! Run," Bones screamed! They ran fast. Bones tried to keep up, jumping over fallen trees maneuvering through the rest. Tommy, on the other hand, was able to go right through them. Even the compass and other items he picked up along the way were going with him. He noticed that the compass went directly through a tree. It seemed anything he was holding could go through objects. "Bones keep up," Tommy shouted! "Don't worry Tommy, I'll catch up. The spider is having more issues then me right now," right as Bones started to speak, the spider jumped into the tree's canopy.

Tommy reached an impasse. He made it to a clearing, but in front of him was a cliff with a river running through it. "Tommy! Tommy! Where are you," Bones yelled? Tommy brightened just enough for Bones to see him. The spider jumped down from the canopy. "Where do we go? Where do we go? Oh, I know, Tommy jump," Bones shouted as he jumped into the river. The cliff was about a fifty-foot drop, and Bones screamed the whole way down until he broke apart in the water. His bones floated because they were so light, and they were so light because he spent a lot of time sunbathing to whiten his bones. Tommy followed Bones' but he did not have to jump. He floated down and tried to find Bones. The white bones were helpful to Tommy because he could see Bones' skull, he picked up the skull. "Tommy, Tommy, are you alright. Hey, you can float! You didn't tell me that. Although you are a ghost, I should have known better. Can you get my skull to shore before the rest of my bones?" Tommy followed the river to a shoreline; it also had a path, so they were cautious of it. Bones was able to move his body in the water. While they were looking for shore, he was able to piece most of himself back together. His body swam to shore.

They moved out from being in the open, hiding behind a bunch of trees. "Which way does the compass point," Bones asked? Tommy opened the compass. "North, directly north," Tommy said. "What, to the castle? You're going to the castle," Bones yelled quietly. "I go to where the compass points me," Tommy said. "That's just our luck. Ok. I can get in through the front door, but you are going to have to find a way in," Bones said. "I think I can go through the wall," Tommy said. "That's good. I'll go to the kitchen. We will regroup there. It's to the left side of the entrance," Bones said. They made their way to the castle, and Tommy took extra care not to be seen by the guards.

Dark Castle

They both reached the kitchen. Tommy opened his compass and went exploring first. Bones made sure he stayed far enough away so they both would not get caught at the same time, if they got caught. The castle was empty, except for some ghosts that stayed within their portraits. The ghosts did not pay mind to Tommy. They were used to skeletons cleaning the castle. Reeds had been in the castle for some time now. He was walking to a study when he noticed a skeleton acting unusual. The skeleton seemed to be following something. Reeds could tell where the skeleton was going and went around to the other side of the castle room. He was about to head the skeleton off when he could see Tommy in the room. He smiled. "It looks like you're back little one," Reeds said.

Tommy walked up to a box on a granite altar. He could tell that it needed a key right away. Tommy looked around, there were some vases and other boxes around the room, so he checked all of them. He found a key. Bones was watching from the second entrance, left of Reeds. Reeds waited until Tommy reached the gem. "That's not going to do," he whispered. Tommy put the key in the box, and a burst of energy shot out, alarming the whole castle. Reeds couldn't wait any longer. He lifted his hand and held Tommy there. Tommy started to get scared again. Reeds came out of the entrance. "I have found you again. I see you are picking up the trades of a thief. It looks like you need to work more on it," he said to Tommy. "You again," Tommy shouted! Bones scrambled out of sight.

"Soon you will be mine," Reeds said. Four guards came in, followed by Narflux and another woman. "Achlys take him to the dungeon," Narflux said. Achlys did not like to be ordered around but put up with it for some strange reason. "I will take him to the cell. Follow," Reeds said. "Tommy was annoyed that his legs would go wherever Reeds would go. Tommy could hear Narflux as they walked out of the room. "Keep that ship here," Narflux command. "I can't. They are the living. The living must leave the island. No living sentinels are allowed except for us. Those have been the rules of the island since I can remember," Achlys said. "Break them," Narflux said. "I can't, you know the dead are, they are very superstitious," she stated. "Then keep the boy here," Narflux shouted. "I can't. I don't know if he is dead or alive. Therefore, the rules force me to banish him from the island," she stated. Achlys didn't want to say much more as she knew Narflux's anger. "Fine, keep them here until I get back," Narflux demanded once again, as he stormed out of the room.

Reeds reached the cell, "in," he said. Tommy went into the cell against his will. "I'm going to find a way out," Tommy said. "I hope you do and find a way onto my team, but you need a key to open this magic cell and I have the only one," Reeds said. He had a smile on his face. Tommy wasn't sure what he was up to but he had a strange feeling about him. "What are you going to do to me," Tommy asked? "It's not me that is going after you, it's Narflux. You stole his gem by his point of view, and you freed his mining operation. He is incredibly angry, and he has a wicked temper too. I'll leave you to think about that," Reeds said as he walked away.

Tommy started looking over the cell. He checked the bars, and they were just as before, it zapped him when he went to touch it. He tried the brick walls, it didn't zap him until he tried to go through it. He looked around the cell to see if there was anything. He noticed a symbol on a brick. He tried to pull the brick out, but he couldn't. It was in there tight. He could not do much more, so he waited trying to figure out what he could do next.

A while later, Bones came walking into the room in front of the cell. "Food, good sir," Bones said. "What are you doing," Tommy asked him? "It's my cover, I'm bringing you food to get you out of here," he opened the small door of the cage. "Ok, let's go," Bones said. "How," Tommy asked? "Go through the opening," Bones told him as he was waiting very impatiently. "Tommy, you're a ghost. You should be able to turn yourself into vaper and float through that opening," Bones said. Tommy tried, but he could not. He didn't know how to turn to vaper much less fit through the small opening that you slide food through. "I don't think it works like that," he said. "Ah, that's the only plan I had," Bones said. "What about a key, can you get that," Tommy asked? "No, I think that man took it with him, but what about a skeleton key," Bones asked? He cupped his hands. He started to separate his hands, and Tommy could see a key starting to form. "Ok, let's try this," Bones said. He stuck the key in the lock and went to twist. "Ahhh," Bones said right before he fell apart. Bones pieced himself back together.

"That is not going to work," Bones said in a loud tone. "Quite Bones, they are going to hear you," Tommy said. "Oh, sorry. What now," Bones asked? "The brick! I got to get that brick out of the wall. I need something to pick at it with," Tommy said. "What about a bone shank," Bones asked? Bones started to make the item. "What's a bone shank," Tommy asked? "It's used to sta… never mind. See if that works," Bones said. Tommy took the shank and picked at the brick until he could pull it out. He looked behind the brick, there was nothing behind it. Tommy looked at the brick, and there were no indications that it could be opened. Tommy thought back to the last time he was in a cage , and he threw the scent sphere at the wall. "This is going to be loud, I think," Tommy said. "Hold on! Let me check the door," Bones said. He poked his head outside the door, there were no guards close to him. "All clear," Bones said as he shut the door again.

Tommy threw the brick at the brick wall, and it broke open. Inside of the crumbled brick, there was a key. He handed the key to Bones. Bones was shaking as he tried to put the key in the lock. He was scared he was going to get zapped again, but he turned the lock, and the cell opened. They snuck past the guards and went back to the room. He crept up to the altar. Bones followed closely behind him. "Bones let me try that key again," Tommy said. Bones handed Tommy the key. Tommy opened the box, and there was the *Diamond of Yew*. He put it in his pocket, but as he did, a burst of energy unleashed. A guard ran up to the entrance. "Stop," one of the guards said. "What do we do, Tommy? We are surrounded," Bones said. Tommy looked but did not see any way out. Just then, a white light shone up from the floor. He could see the symbol on the tile. "Go to the symbol," Tommy yelled. Tommy ran through the light. He was surrounded by a brightly lit area as far as he could see. Tommy found himself standing on a stone pad with the symbol under him. He had no clue how he ended up there, but at least he was away from that dreadful place and the guards. There were people in white cloaks around him. There were six of them. He could tell by their voices, who some of them were. He had met or ran into all of them, at some point. He could see they were surrounding him. "What did you do to Bones," Tommy shouted? "He's safe, at least for the time being, but we don't have much time. He's where you're going next," Reeds said. "Who are all of you," he asked? Bashiri spoke, "you can call us the *Six Cloaks*. We can't let you disappear. You have a future to see to," Bashiri stated to Tommy. "There may come a time when you are needed. Will you call to arms or will you lay hidden away," Ayla asked?

"What is it you are looking for," Reeds questioned? "What do you mean," Tommy asked them? "If you could have anything you want, wealth, power, the ability to lock someone up and throw away the key," Reeds said to him. "My sister," Tommy said without hesitation. "Is that all you want," Bashiri asked? "If it's a choice between my family and my life, then I choose my family," Tommy stated. "Then it has been decided," Reeds said. "Find the key," the sixth member said as a big white light flashed around Tommy. All of a sudden, he found himself outside of the camp next to Bones, who was already scouting.

Back at the *Six Cloaks*. Achlys spoke, "do you think he's ready for the Misty Vails?" There was complete silence as they all started to wonder. "Do you think he is the one," Ayla asked the others? "Maybe, only time will tell," Bashiri said. "Do you think he's righteous," Achlys asked? "Let's hope he will be a benevolent one," Reeds said. "And if not," Achlys asked again? "Then may the Gods have mercy on our souls," Reeds finished the conversation.

Chapter 10

Piece 7

The Escape

"Bones, what's going on," Tommy asked? "Tommy, there you are! What took you so long," Bones asked? "I met with six cloaked people all in white, and I think I know almost all of them," Tommy said. "You saw the *Six Cloaks*. No one ever gets to meet the *Six Cloaks*. What did they want," Bones asked? "I don't know, they asked me what I wanted, but we don't have time for that," Tommy said. "Right, where do we go next," Bones asked? "We have to go back to the Cap'n and see if they escaped," Tommy said. They crept back to the cage and found the crew again.

"Cap'n, I got the *Diamond of Yew*," Tommy whispered. "Good lad, we were just about to break out of here," the Cap'n said. "So, what's the plan," Bones asked? "Who are you," Sarrah asked? "Bones Weary, I'm with Tommy," Bones said. She looked at Tommy. "I made a new friend. He helped me get the gem," Tommy said. Sarrah looked at Bones again. "Help me get off this Island, and I will give you whatever you want," Bones said. "Fair enough for me. Glad to make ye acquaintance Mr. Weary," the Cap'n anouncced . "Please, call me Bones," Bones told them. "The plan was to wait until they unlock the cage, and then we be goin' to fight our way out," the Cap'n said. "Unarmed," Bones asked?

"Don't ye know a pirate is never unarmed, but we do have to wait for the key," the Cap'n said. "The key! That's it, don't forget the key," Tommy pulled the key he got from the cell out. He put the key in the lock ever so slowly and twisted. The lock unlocked, and the cell door opened. "Is that a magic key," Bones asked? The Cap'n with a grin said, "it looks to be a magic key. Good lad, ye came back with two magical items." He then looked at Bones, "maybe three," he finished.

"Ok, ye have yer back up weapons," the Cap'n asked? All but Isabel, Tommy, and Bones pulled out their hidden weapons. Tommy looked at Bones and asked, "what about your bone shank?" "Ah-ha, I got something bigger and better. A bone club. Cool huh," Bones asked? The Cap'n saw Bones' weapon. He looked at his little dagger and then looked at the bone club and asked, "ye don't suppose ye can make one fer me crew, do ye?" "I got one better; I can make anything out of bone. What type of weapons do you want," Bones asked? In five minutes, he made their weapons: a bone hammer for the Cap'n, bone staffs for Robert and Joseph, Martin asked for a tall bone sword, Sarrah asked for a bone club and then asked for bone shields for the kids. Bones handed the last one to Tommy. He took the shield and tied it on the back of Isabel. "Now she's protected from both sides," he said. "But what about you," Bones asked? "I have a better plan," Tommy said.

"Sarrah, take the kids to a safe spot. Robert, Joseph go around back and get our weapons, don't ferget any one of them. Martin ye come with me, we be goin' to make a distraction with those barrels over there," the Cap'n directed. Martin and the Cap'n snuck to the gun powder barrels, while

Robert and Joseph went to the back of the tent where they saw them take their weapons in. Martin grabbed a pouch of gun powder and laid it to the tree line where the Cap'n was. The Cap'n waited. Robert and Joseph noticed there was a guard in the tent. Joseph crept in and ever so quietly lifted his staff and knocked the skeleton guard's head off. He held the mouth shut while Robert strapped as many weapons as he could carry. Robert switched places with Joseph. Joseph started to strap the weapons on, when they heard a loud explosion. By this point, Joseph had grabbed the last weapon. "Times up Joseph, we have to go," Robert said. "That's the last of them. Let's go," Joseph replied. Robert took the head and stuffed it in a box.

Skeleton guards started to go after all of them. Robert and Joseph had four guards chasing them. Tommy raced to Joseph, who was having the most problems. Tommy knelt behind one of the guards. Joseph saw what Tommy was doing and pushed the guard so he fell over Tommy. Tommy pulled off the guard's head and tossed it to Joseph. While it was in the air, he kicked the skull making the skull fly far away. Tommy went back to Isabel who was getting attacked. Guards were attacking all three; Sarrah, Bones, and little Isabel when Tommy picked up a shield he found lying on the ground and rammed it into the guard. The guard fell over, and Isabel kicked the skull. Unfortunately, it did not go far, but Tommy had a plan. He grabbed both guard's tibia bones and put them in a barrel and closed the lid.

The Cap'n and Martin ran to the others. The Cap'n was going to help Sarrah, but by the time he had got there, the guard was nothing but a pile of bones thoroughly dismantled. The crew all met up with Sarrah, Isabel, Tommy, and Bones. Bones was never given a command, except by Sarrah, who told him to follow them and thankfully he did. These skeleton guards where unlike Bones. He could put his bones back together faster than them, but there were more guards.

They raced back to the ship. Fortunately, the guards were overconfident about their abilities and only left a few guards to guard the ship. They made their way to the skiff, and there were guards standing around it, four of them. All at once, the Cap'n, Martin, Robert, and Joseph charged in and knocked off the heads of the skeleton guards. The rest grabbed their heads and threw them in the water. Bones being a little different from the guards, liked to sunbathe making his bones lighter. However, the guards bones sank to the bottom of the sea. They all boarded the skiff and rowed back to the ship.

"It's about time you made it back to the ship. We were playing hide and seek with the skeletons," Dr. Craze said once the Cap'n climbed on board. Bones was last to board. He stepped onto the ship, and he could hear a growl. "Aye, you have a dog, Tommy," he asked in a panicked voice! "That's Bahrk, my dog," Tommy said. "Don't you know that dogs are a skeletons worst opponent, they like bones," Bones said. "He sure liked the skeletons that came on board. Thanks to him, we were able to fight off the guards and throw them overboard," William replied gratefully. "The dog made a great distraction. Thank you for leaving him," Dr. Craze handed Bahrk a cracker, and Bahrk ate it. Some of the crumbles fell out of Bahrk's stomach. "At least I know my bones will fall out of him if he eats them," Bones said as Bahrk came to sniff him. "Curses for taking tremendous care of my bones. Ahh, Tommy. Get him away," Bones said. "Come on boy, let's go over here," Tommy said to Bahrk.

"Martin set sail as fast as ye can," the Cap'n commanded. "Which way sir," Martin asked? "East. Warn me of any danger," the Cap'n announced. Once they reached lighter skies, the Cap'n directed Martin and the crew to watch for danger. "Tommee with me," the Cap'n said. Tommy followed the Cap'n into his quarters. "Can I have the gem me lad," the Cap'n asked? Tommy pulled out the gem and handed it to the Cap'n. "That's not the *Diamond of Yew*. It's red like the *Ruby of Fire*," the Cap'n was deep in thought. "Do you think they accidentally mixed up the gems," Tommy asked? "No, they did it on purpose. I'm sorry lad, we must wait until we get the last gem, the real *Diamond of Yew*. If we have the *Ruby of Fire*, then they must have crossed gems in the book. So, the *Ruby of Fire* should be the *Diamond of Yew* in the book," the Cap'n assumed. "We will see where color patterns from the book gets us when we go lookin' fer the *Ruby of Fire*."

The Cap'n rearranged the gems in the compass for the coordinates listed under the *Ruby of Fire*. He finished, and the compass had a new direction. He brought it to Martin. Tommy followed the Cap'n. Martin changed course, but the compass stayed in the same direction until the ship came about in a full circle. "Cap'n, there is something wrong with the compass. It stays in line with the ship no matter what direction I point the ship in," Martin said. "No, the compass is not broken. Let me see that," the Cap'n stated. Martin handed the compass back to the Cap'n. He had an idea. The Cap'n walked along the ship to see when it would change.

"The gem be on the ship! The question be where," the Cap'n announced. "Cap'n, can I look for it," Tommy asked? The Cap'n handed the compass to Tommy. Tommy moved to the bow of the ship until it turned in the opposite direction. "I think it is under us," Tommy said. Tommy went to the haul of the ship, where the crew's hammocks where. He reached his hammock, and it pointed to the box that the Oracle had given him. He grabbed the box and raced back to the Cap'n. "Cap'n it is in here," Tommy announced. The Cap'n took the compass back and verified something was in the box that the compass was pointing to. "It's locked lad, how are we goin' to get in it? We still need the key," the Cap'n said. Bones was enthralled with the hunt and spoke up, "maybe not, you said the key Tommy had was a magic key correct? Maybe it will open the box too." Tommy pulled out his key again and put it in the lock of the box, he turned the key and the box opened. Inside was the last gem they were looking for, the true *Diamond of Yew*.

The Cap'n and Tommy went back to the captain's quarters and rearranged the compass again. This time it was in a fixed position heading towards the *Locket of Two - Blue Diamond,* the second half of the neckless. The first half of the *Locket of Two - Purple Diamond,* was the one that Isabel now owned. Just then, they heard cannon fire. The Cap'n came racing out of his quarters. "Martin, what be goin' on out here," the Cap'n demanded. "We are being chased," Martin replied. "Full speed ahead," the Cap'n ordered. The *Night Drifter* pulled further away from the ship and out of the line of fire of the cannons. The attacking ship was still following. The Cap'n pulled out his telescope. "That's not good. Narflux is following us," he told whoever was nearby. Tommy, who was holding the compass noticed they were going in the wrong direction, but he had an idea, and so did the Cap'n. Tommy handed the compass to the Cap'n. "We are going in the wrong direction," Tommy said. Cap'n Samm took the compass and made his plan. "Martin, go northeast for about an hour. We should be able to outrun them until then," he said.

An hour's time past, and it was time for the Cap'n to put his plan into action. "Martin, it's time to dive," the Cap'n announced. The original crew had experienced it, but for the new members well, they had no idea the ship could dive under the water. Robert activated the amulet, and the ship dove under the water. Cap'n Samm patiently waited until Martin settled the ship under the water. "Martin, follow the compass," Cap'n Samm gave the compass to Martin. Martin turned the ship in the southeast direction. They sailed underwater until the Cap'n felt it was safe. "Surface the ship," he ordered. The ship came up out of the water. The crew searched for the attacking ship, but the ship was nowhere. "Good job me mateys! Let's make way fer the next destination," Cap'n Samm said. The crew cheered!

The Other Neckless

They approached Read's Island and started to move past it until Martin noticed that the compass was pointing to it. He circled the island until he was able to find a harbor. Read's Island was a big trade port with lots of three-story homes lining the streets. "Alright me boy, it's time to find the second part of the *Locket of Two - Blue Diamond*. Now, I don't know what we will find, but with any luck ye may find that sister of yer's," said Cap'n Samm. "Thank you for looking so long for my sister," Tommy replied.

The Cap'n inhaled and took to one knee, "Tommee, I have to let ye know, we may not find ye sister, but I will keep lookin' fer her, as well as Sarrah." Tommy looked down at the floorboards. His mind was racing. He had many questions, and then he remembered that he found the Cap'n. "Even if we don't find her, I will continue to look too," Tommy said. "That's me boy. Let's find ye special treasure," Cap'n Samm said. Sarrah was on looking and tearing up. She couldn't bear the thought of Tommy's heartbreaking. Before they got off the ship, she went to Tommy. "Never give up Tommy," she said. She smiled at him, hugged him, and sent him on his way."

Tommy walked the streets with the Cap'n. He could see the red bricks that paved the streets, which would typically fascinate him, but he was still looking down, wondering what he would find. Cap'n Samm looked over at him. "Tommee, this is your quest, so ye should hold the compass," Cap'n Samm suggested. Tommy took the compass and looked at the colorful gems inside the compass. He took a deep breath and said, "this is it," and he started coordinating himself with the compass. It didn't take long, Tommy was moving fast, so fast that the Cap'n had a hard time keeping up with him. "Slow down Tommee, don't go off all on ye own," Cap'n Samm shouted to him. Tommy sprinted about ten blocks. He turned the corner and saw a tan cloaked figure on a narrow street that was just big enough for a wagon. A wagon that cut him off before he could reach the intersection. He would have to back out, so he decided to go around the block. The Cap'n had just caught up to him when Tommy turned right and continued going faster.

"Tommee, where ye goin' now me lad," Cap'n Samm asked as he tried to keep up with Tommy? Tommy made his way to the next block, and found the cloaked figure again, and this time she was going straight away from him. Tommy was coming up behind the cloaked figure before it could make another turn. He stopped the cloaked figure and said, "wait, are you my sister?" She took off her hood, she had long blonde hair and blue eyes, just like Tommy. "Do you have the *Blue Diamond Locket*," he tried again. She looked at him funny. "I'm sorry, I had a brother, but he died, it was a long time ago, and I don't know what the *Blue Diamond* is." That's the *Locket of Two*," Tommy said. She pulled out her locket and opened it up. The locket had been damaged, and she could barely make out his picture. "I'm fifteen, how are you so young," she said? "Truth is, I did die. I'm a ghost, but I found my sister, and now we can be a family," Tommy exclaimed. It was ironic that his younger sister became his older sister, but he didn't care about that. He was excited to see her.

"I'm sorry Tommy, I can't go. I live at an orphanage, and I was told I'm un-adoptable," she said. "What? Take me to whoever told ye this child. Un-adoptable, that's absurd," the Cap'n exclaimed. She walked him to the orphanage. He charged in and found the headmaster. "I demand to know who said that this little," he stopped and looked at her, "what's ye name me dear?" "Allie, Allison sir," she said. "Why can I not adopt Allison," he demanded? "You're a pirate, you can't adopt, but if you give me an hour, I will summon the master," she said. Unbeknownst to the Cap'n, the headmaster was told to summon the master if anyone asked for her. An hour went by, and as promised, a man in a nice black suit came out wearing a purple shirt with a dark purple tie. "Reeds, it's you," Tommy rushed at him as if he were going to knock him over. "Hold on Tommy, if you want your sister, then you will hear me out in private," Reeds said, as he looked at Cap'n Samm. "Just you," he stated again. Tommy stopped halfway to him. He wanted to beat him up so badly, but he knew that wouldn't give him his sister. "Fine, I will listen, and then I'm going to beat you up," Tommy said. Reeds chuckled a little and then rolled his eyes. "This way please, I'm a terribly busy man," Reeds said.

They walked into a well-supplied library with red leather chairs and dark mahogany bookshelves. "Now Tommy, tell me what you want, and before you say anything think about it very carefully," Reeds said. "I want my sister," Tommy said. "Is that all you want," Reeds replied? Tommy stopped when he heard Reeds respond. "You're one of the *Six Cloaks*," he said. "Yes, but everything comes at a price," Reeds said. He pulled out a ship, Tommy's ship. The one Oscar's assistant gave him. "How do you have my ship," Tommy asked? "That wasn't the only thing I gave you," Reeds said as he leaned over to Tommy. His face started to age older until he looked like the assistant. Tommy was going to speak when he thought back to another strange time in Atlantia. "You're one of Bashiri's servants too," he said.

"That's not how you barter Tommy, I was saving your sister for the right person," Reeds said.

"Then what do you want," he asked Reeds? "Let's keep the *Six Cloaks* and all you know about me a secret from the world, and in return, I will let your Cap'n adopted little Allie," he said. "How did you do all of this?" "I look after many people, not just your sister but my daughter Julia, Oscar's wife and I would really like to keep them a secret for as long as I can." "But you locked me up twice," Tommy said. "I couldn't help it. I wanted you to meet your sister as fast as you could, so I brought you to the cave where the Cap'n could find you. In the *Dark Castle*, it was the only way for you to get the key without me blowing my cover," Reeds said. Tommy thought long and hard but thought if he was that kind old assistant who he admired so much, maybe Reeds wasn't so bad either. Reeds already knew what he was going to do and started pulling out a rolled document on a high shelf. "I'll do it. I will keep your secrets, secrets for my sister. Reeds smiled as he pulled out the document.

"I guess you should get your Cap'n then," Reeds said as he opened the adoption document for Allison and placed it in front of Tommy. Tommy got up and opened the door, calling for the Cap'n. "Normally, we don't let pirates adopt, but she has been here for so long," Reeds said to Cap'n Samm. "What will it be," the Cap'n asked. "The Compass," Reeds replied. "I'm sorry, I have already promised that to another, and a Cap'n can't break his honor," Cap'n Samm said. "I know. I will be in touch," Reeds said. The Cap'n look at him dumbfounded. "Does everyone know about the compass," Cap'n Samm asked? "Pretty much, now sign here," Reeds said. The Cap'n signed the papers. "Congratulations! You have officially adopted Allison. Now, if you don't mind getting her stuff and moving along, I'm a remarkably busy man," Reeds said.

Allison, who had been outside in a panic, looked at Cap'n Samm. "Me dear, me crew has just adopted ye," Allison screamed, started to cry and then ran over to the Cap'n and hugged him. She then walked to Tommy and knelt down and gave him the biggest hug of all. "You should meet our new family," Tommy said.

They made it back to the ship with Allie's stuff, which wasn't much, but they had already had more then she could ever imagine. Along the way, Cap'n Samm bought everything she had ever wanted in town through the window; a nice dress, chocolate, and a necklace set without the ruby. Tommy asked the Cap'n why he didn't buy the ruby. Cap'n Samm replied that he had a better one than that. They stopped by one particular store, a toy store, and inside the shop owner gave her a crafted doll that he had been saving for her when she got adopted.

When Isabel saw her, she shrieked at the top of her lungs. Sarrah and the rest of the crew ran to Isabel and stopped when they saw the Cap'n. "Is it true," Sarrah asked? "Say hello to your new crewmate, Allison. Allie, for short," Cap'n Samm announced. "I thought she was going to be a bit younger, like six years old," Martin said. Robert and Joseph were too stunned to say anything. "I guess Tommee has been a ghost a lot longer than we thought," the Cap'n replied. "Can I play with your doll," Isabel asked? "Why don't we play together," Allie said. Isabel shrieked again and grabbed her by the hand and took Allie to her favorite spot on the ship. Tommy walked on the ship. Cap'n Samm stopped him, "ye done well, me lad." Tommy smiled in satisfaction.

They restocked the next day. Bones went to the Cap'n, "it looks like I'll be off. "Hold up, why don't ye become a part of the crew until we find a command center," the Cap'n said. "You mean that," Bones asked? "Ye can pay me off slowly for the deal when we met. It may take some time to find a place to fit all of us," Cap'n Samm said. "Thank you Cap'n," Bones said and ran to tell Tommy, he was on the bow of the deck floating above playing with Isabel while Allie watched. Tommy came down when he heard Bones call for him, and Isabel followed. Sarrah was watching from afar. "Tommy, the Cap'n has allowed me to stay on the ship," Bones said. Tommy stopped to think about what the Cap'n would say, and from his heart, he replied, "of course, you're family. He hugged bones and started flying again. Isabel followed.

"Tommee," the Cap'n called, he had panic in his voice. This time the Cap'n went to them. "How is Isabel flying," Cap'n Samm asked? "I gave her my ring," he said. "But so aren't ye," Cap'n Samm said. "I don't know," Tommy said. Just then, Allie had an idea. "Tommy, can you come down," she asked? Tommy went to her. "I want to give you this since you gave the other one to Isabel," Allie said. She put it around his neck, and he started to glow brightly. He hovered a few feet off the ground, turning into a living boy. "Tommy," Sarrah shrieked. The loudest the crew had ever heard as she ran to him. She wrapped her arms around him and said, "my baby boy." Tears of joy flowed down her face.

By this time, the entire crew was weeping, and the men couldn't hold back their tears either. After they had summoned up their strength, the crew set sail. Allie turned to Robert, "is it always like this?" "Yup," Robert replied. Allie started to sing while the crew listened. *"I'm all set to leave the wagon. "I'm all set to go astray. Oh, bur dance. I will leave the shore. To find what I've been longing for. The Day I return, a hero I shall be."*